SEDONA DRAGONS

by Robert Louis DeMayo

Sedona Dragons

2

Robert Louis DeMayo

This is a work of Fiction

I'm gonna say it again. This is all fiction. Made up. The locations are real... the restaurants, the events, even some of the people... BUT none of them were ever in any of the scenes that take place in this book. I'm just trying to prevent the story from turning into a conspiracy theory.

Then again, it's a Sedona story, so I'm sure it will eventually take on a life of its own – and that could mean just about anything.

This book is dedicated to,

Frankie

Coffeepot Rock

Table of Contents

Coyote

MONDAY

Prologue

Eleven Eleven

Louis hates crowds. They make him feel like he's imploding. He dislikes being around big groups, even if they are all friends. He prefers the woods or the desert, places with breathing room. That probably doesn't surprise you, I'm sure, as most fifty-nine-year-old artists tend to be reclusive.

On nights like this, a few hours before 11:11 PM on 11/11, even normally quiet places like Sedona's Amitabha Stupa and Peace Park can get overrun with people, but that's a lot of ones and tough to resist for some. The Park closes at dusk, but astrologers love the 11/11 or 12/12 dates and flock to Sedona then, more than willing to sneak in. They refer to these dates as manifestation portals or energetic gateways.

When Louis sees all the cars parked on the street, he drives right by and doesn't stop until he is heading towards the western canyons.

"Adios, my friends," he snickers, "I know where you all won't be."

The full moon won't rise for a few nights, but it's getting close to full now as it hovers over Louis' bone-white Buick

Enclave, peering at him from a safe distance—as if even the moon can sense his agitation.

He follows Dry Creek Road west, amidst imposing red and yellow cliffs, eventually turning off to take Boynton Pass by Doe Mesa, where the road turns to dirt.

He barely slows when it does, barreling ahead like the days when he drove jeep tours. The Buick rattles and groans as it cruises over potholes and through fine red dust, kicking up clouds in its wake.

At one point, he passes a man standing alone in the dark. He's wearing a gun at his hip, and he's perched in front of a closed gate. The guy glares at him like a guard dog, and Louis thinks, here's another guy not willing to share the night.

The road is a mess, and Louis knows the Buick will pay for it later, but on this night, he doesn't care. He plows ahead recklessly. A few miles later, he parks on Bradshaw Hill, where there's a nice view of Mingus Mountain to the west; the lights of Jerome twinkle in the distance.

The insects have died off for the year, and the lack of crickets or cicadas is noticeable. There is a gap in the night yearning to be filled despite the bright moon. Usually, Louis would welcome an evening like this—but tonight, he's restless. He's an introvert and not interested in the limelight unless it's necessary to market a book. As an author, that's when he must suck it up and smile.

He even gives talks at the local high school. The kids seemed to enjoy his rambling performance once he switches to stories about animal encounters; after all, what teenager doesn't want to hear a story about getting chased by an elephant or charged by a mountain gorilla?

Yet even those stories lack something. They are missing a fragment of the truth. He feels the need to make the students see all sides of a story, not just the exciting moments. He wants them to be angry and fearful as much as excited; after all, only those who experience sunburn truly respect the sun.

And there's a lot to be angry about these days, not just the world outside – politics, climate change, etc. – it seems a dark element has entered his Sedona bubble. It takes over his mind for a moment, and then he lets it pass, returning to think about the students.

Is it wrong that he wishes they could suffer like he did? Or worry? Probably, they've got enough on their plate, but still, he has to point the finger at something... or someone.

He likes even less being respected. The term "Sir" irks him. Maybe a slight recognition of his writing isn't a bad thing, but this "respectable" thing drives him mad. He detests the students thinking he's figured it all out, that he has any practical answers – he doesn't – only stories, and those have been filtered for public consumption. They say every sinner has a future, and every saint has a past, but nobody recognizes that maybe those evil deeds, mistakes or destructive behaviors are part of what makes us. He hates it when someone comments on another and says, "That's a red flag!"

We're all just a collection of red flags. Most people are just too tired to keep flying them.

Maybe that's what fuels that unbearable suffering – the weight of life. But what drives certain people to do things that make others suffer? Why be mean or hurtful? He's heard rumors lately, in Sedona, of someone who is hurtful. Someone that needs to be stopped – but who's gonna do it?

He sits on the hood of his Buick and takes out a plastic container. Opening it reveals about three grams of mushrooms that have been soaked in honey. The contents have turned blue over the last three months, and Louis had just about forgotten this gift he picked up at the last Grateful Dead show, down in Phoenix.

Another FINAL concert for the immortal band.

He eats the entire batch – including slurping up the honey – while scanning the horizon for UFOs, which are sighted almost nightly out here by surveillance groups.

Gotta love Sedona. You'd think by the number of sightings out here that the aliens have an aircraft carrier parked somewhere. He's been told it's invisible. Ha.

After about ten minutes, he drinks a whole jug of water, locks his car, and sticks the keys above the front right tire.

A pack of coyotes sing out to the east, and he walks in that direction. The stars float above him, suddenly taking on a wavy air, and the constellations he knows slide forward.

The moon has shifted drastically in the sky when Louis next comes around. He senses some time has passed, mainly from the tired ache in his limbs. He's been walking in a trance for seemingly forever, but a noise has pulled him from his daze.

Someone screamed. He heard it clearly, even in his stupor.

He listens now, but there is nothing. An owl hoots.

Could it have been in my head? He wonders.

In the near distance, he sees a light and moves toward it.

It's a vehicle. A truck with the high beams on. They are pointed at what appears to be a recently filled-in grave.

Someone stands over the pile of dirt and yells.

"Serves you right!"

There's something wrong with this scene, and Louis slinks away. In his haste, he stumbles and nearly falls headfirst into an agave, its sharp spikes threatening to impale him.

Later, Louis finds himself picking his way through a field of prickly pear cactus. He's on a deer trail, so there is a path, but the mushrooms have kicked in, and things are a bit fuzzy.

He's mumbling a song. It's an old Grateful Dead tune-- actually a cover of a swamp-blues classic recorded initially by Slim Harpo--but there's nobody within miles who would recognize it.

He shouts out the chorus, *"I'm a King Bee baby... buzzing 'round your hive!"*

18

He pauses to catch his breath, and suddenly someone shouts out. He glances around, confused.

"When were you born?!" yells a voice emanating from underneath a juniper where the shadows still linger.

Instantly, Louis perks up. "I was born ninety-nine years after the Civil War ended and almost a year to the day after President Kennedy was shot."

A hippie steps into the moonlight and shrugs.

"I don't care about that stuff, man... don't you have a birthday coming up?"

Louis focuses and sees that he knows the man.

Joey, about twenty-nine, is indeed a hippie, and on this evening, he looks a little feral. He goes by Coyote, which tonight seems appropriate.

He stands there in faded jeans that have been cut away just above the knees and a leather vest that leaves his scrawny chest exposed. A worn red bandana circles his forehead and keeps his greasy blond hair in place.

Louis has no idea what he is doing alone in the high desert.

Joey doesn't seem surprised to see Louis stumbling along, alone and clearly high.

Louis grins. "I do—in ten days, I'll be sixty."

Joey nods. "We need to smoke on that."

It takes a few more minutes for Louis to navigate through the cacti to the juniper, and by the time he sits down, Joey has lit a joint. Light blue berries litter the ground around them.

For only a few seconds, Louis hesitates. "Maybe I shouldn't... I'm cruising along pretty good right now."

Joey stares into his eyes and asks, "Mushrooms?" and Louis nods.

Joey shrugs. "This will level you out."

Louis takes a few pulls off the joint and exhales. Despite the waxing moon, the stars above them seem exceptionally brilliant tonight.

The smoke has a strange taste, and Louis comments on it.

Joey nods, "My bad—I should have mentioned I ground up a peyote bud with it."

Louis nods and grunts, but his mind is spinning.

Suddenly, he stands, shudders uncontrollably, and walks into the desert.

Joey shrugs and mutters, "You're welcome."

Sometime later, Louis comes around again to find himself stumbling along a dirt road. He dimly recognizes a few of the rocks on the horizon, gets himself oriented and begins to walk east, but within a few minutes, he hears an engine and stops.

He waits until a yellow jeep approaches. It's a modified Rubicon with the back blown out to carry passengers. It's well past sunset, and Louis can't imagine what the driver is doing out here at this hour. Without a good excuse, not only could the driver get fired, but the company could lose its permit and be out of business.

He recognizes the driver and smiles at him.

"Hey Jimmy," he says, "got room for a passenger?"

Jimmy is a silver-haired Sioux. A former bull rider, he still proudly wears the belt buckle.

"Sure," he says, "I can do that. But you know them Barbies would never pick you up—day or night."

He's referring to the Pink Jeeps, which are run by a more corporate company. To be fair, none of them are supposed to pick up hitchhikers, but they will all stop if they think you need help. The Arizona heat takes no prisoners, and jeep drivers know that.

When they are moving again, Jimmy says, "I saw that big bull again earlier tonight."

20

Louis shrugs. For years, Jimmy has claimed he periodically runs into a massive, white Brahma bull that haunts this area. Nobody else has ever seen it, and the other guides tease him, saying he's having bull-riding flashbacks.

When they reach the end of the dirt road, Jimmy stops and puts the jeep in park. The engine pings while they sit in silence.

"This is as far as I go, Pilgrim," he says, doing his best John Wayne accent.

Louis nods. For some reason, it makes perfect sense.

He gets out and shakes Jimmy's hand. "Thanks, brother!" he shouts.

As the jeep drives away, Louis pauses for a minute, confused because even in his trance-like state, he knows Jimmy has been dead for almost a year now.

To his right, Cockscomb Butte lies bathed in moonlight, and he drifts that way. A trail winds up the side of the butte, and he slowly ascends.

About half an hour later, a voice echoes hauntingly off the towering red walls of stone. It's slow, as if the singer is out of breath.

"I'm a King... Bee... baby... "

Heavy breathing.

"Buzzin' round... your hive."

He shouts something incoherent, and then his laughter bounces off the walls.

Suddenly, a roar shatters the night.

Louis screams once, quickly, and the night snuffs out any further sounds.

Cockscomb Butte

TUESDAY

Chapter One

Fire

Nicola woke in the night from a troubling dream. She turned on a soft light on the end table and drank her night water while she let it replay. There weren't a lot of images, just darkness and a deep sense of dread. Yet she somehow sensed something disturbing had happened to a friend — that he was connected to this horrible dream — and he wasn't in a good place.

Her heart raced, and she knew she wouldn't fall asleep again until she got some answers.

She eventually dialed a number and listened as it went to voicemail, then hung up without leaving a message. If he were okay, he would see she called, but a rumbling in her gut told her he wasn't okay at all.

For another few minutes, she sat there thinking, and then, with a sigh, she got up. She was forty-eight and not impulsive, but she knew she had no choice but to drive north. She was currently in Mesa, a good two hours from Sedona, but there would be no traffic at this hour, and she hoped to be there by sunrise.

She left Mesa and passed through Phoenix quietly, stopping only once to grab a coffee at the Starbucks drive-through—one of her few remaining vices. If she had been home, she would have made a chai—better and cheaper than what they served at Starbucks—but a black Americano for the road was what she craved right now.

Her brain was still sleepy, and she needed to focus.

She carefully sipped the hot coffee as she drove through the night. To the east, the horizon was beginning to lighten, and by the time the sun glinted into view, she'd left the saguaros and entered the high desert.

Nicola had a few dark moments in her past, but they were mostly behind her. Now, thanks to finding her bliss in astrology and energy work, like Reiki, she walked through life with purpose and high self-esteem. Her friends and clients thought she was a force.

Her body was covered in numerous tattoos, which confused some men because it made them think she was vulnerable, which was far from the truth. This misperception allowed her to, at times, seize opportunities. Most men never glimpsed the fire within her, too caught up in their own drama; but if they crossed her, they paid the price.

By the time she reached the Verde Valley, the coffee was long gone. It had woken her some, but she still fought to stifle a few yawns.

She'd gone up in elevation on this journey, rising from 1,200 feet in Mesa to around 4,600 feet in Sedona. The vegetation had changed on the ride, first leaving the cholla and ironwood trees and then the saguaros.

Now, she saw high desert vegetation with bushes like manzanita and scrub oak taking root along the highway. Small clusters of pinion pine and juniper began to fill the hillsides, and in the distance, she could glimpse ponderosa pines on the top of the ridges.

She thought of the friend she was worried about and a few other Sedona guys she had known over the years and smiled.

These Sedona guys were all "new." They radiated innocence, a lot of them because they'd just tuned into so many things: meditation, ecstatic dance and yoga, the ego, toxic masculinity, etc. Some improved themselves, others became instant gurus or shamans—falling victim to the very thing they'd been trying to extinguish, the ego—and others basically got chased out of town because nobody wanted to deal with their toxic karma.

People joke about places like Sedona "kicking" or "spitting" you out, but it's the truth; if you don't fit in, you won't last long. It's as simple as that. Well, maybe. Sometimes the energy kicks you out, sometimes you get a little nudge from residents.

She took the Camp Verde exit onto Rte. 260, and after passing through Cottonwood, she glimpsed Sedona's famous sandstone cliffs. She also spotted four hot air balloons slowly cruising by, their baskets filled with gawking tourists.

Hot Yoga, in the Bashas parking lot, had just opened the doors, although the first class wouldn't begin for another half hour.

Nicola entered and was greeted by the owner, Jenn.

She paid for the morning class, grabbed a mat and towel, and then took a warm shower. By the time others began to show up, she was lying on the mat, waiting.

Eventually, about thirty-five people filled the room, most of them women. A low murmur of whispered conversation floated through the room until Jenn cleared her voice.

Jenn said, "Good morning, everyone. Thank you for showing up and making an effort. We will begin in Mountain Pose."

A few smiled back as they stood. For many, this was a highlight of their day. The room was typically heated to between 95 and 100 degrees, which isn't super-hot—especially for Arizonans—but as she talked, Jenn walked around with a mist bottle, continuously spraying. As she increased the humidity in the room, the heat felt more oppressive.

Jenn continued, "Eckhart Tolle said, 'Realize deeply that the present moment is all you ever have. Make the Now the primary focus of your life.'"

About a quarter of the people in the room were tourists; the others were locals. Some were retired, and the rest were massage therapists, cooks, waiters, store clerks, tour guides, and even leftover psychics from the 1990s. Most knew each other, and these women were up on the latest gossip—which was one of the reasons why Nicola had taken the class.

Jenn exhaled and said, "Downward dog."

She didn't follow her own instructions but instead walked around the room between mats and continued her narration. Now that people were exerting themselves, the room heated up even more, and within a few minutes, everyone was drenched in sweat.

"Or, as I like to say, 'It's a good day to have a good day.'"

Nicola struggled slightly to control her breathing. The morning hot yoga flow was the same routine every day, and those who took it a few times a week were familiar with it, but it was a challenge if it was new to you. She slowed, rather than fighting to keep up, and eventually found her rhythm.

The women on the mats around her had a glow about them. They were all fit, with toned muscles, pumping lungs, and flushed faces. Sweat drained off their glistening bodies in buckets and drenched the mats, most of which had a towel or cloth on them to soak up some of the moisture.

At the end of ninety minutes, everyone collapsed into sivasina, where they were told they could remain for up to ten minutes until the next class started.

Nicola lay there with her eyes closed, listening, while most of the class stirred, rolling up their mats and wiping away puddles of the perspiration they'd created. A few talked loudly despite the rule not to, now that Jenn had left the room.

To her right, two women whispered, and Nicola opened her ears when she heard her friend's name. "I thought Louis was supposed to be here this morning," said one.

"He was. Aside from those dances he's obsessed with, this is one of his few social events... not like him to miss this class," the other replied.

The first one added, "Last I heard, he was heading off with some mushrooms on some kind of vision quest, so who knows where he is."

"That man needs to grow up," said her friend.

Their flippant attitude bothered Nicola because she feared the worst. She still sensed a darkness around him.

When she passed the front desk, she overheard gossip about a missing person, but it was a younger guy, and Jenn didn't seem to approve of him.

She said, "I hired him to do some work, and he never showed — doesn't surprise me. Just as well, I'd rather not have him around the girls."

In the parking lot, Nicola tried Louis's cell phone again. This time, she left a message, then drove to his home, which was nearby.

She wasn't surprised when his car wasn't there.

Nicola wished she knew where Louis had gone. She wasn't afraid to take a risk and search on her own — but where? She was going to have to dig deeper.

Chapter Two

Earth

Selena sat with a client in the "enchanted" garden patio at The Chocola Tree Organic Oasis restaurant. She had picked a secluded table in the corner because of the privacy and low lighting. The two had been working together for a while, dealing with the young woman's trauma, but currently, they were simply enjoying a meal together, trying to lighten up before saying goodbye.

A Kirtan artist was performing traditional Sanskrit mantras—with a modern twist—while to his left, a young woman was suspended in the air as she completed a daring move on an aerial silk rig.

Her client watched the woman on the silk rig twirling through space, but she wasn't seeing her. Her eyes were sunken into her head, and she looked dehydrated. "You should drink some water," said Selena, "you look parched."

The woman nodded and took a small sip. There were bruises on her neck that she tried to conceal with a silk scarf, but when she swallowed, they crept around the soft material and glared at Selena like an accusation.

Selena was thirty-six, ten years older than her client, but she felt much older than that today. Some of the issues she dealt with were heavy; lately, she had difficulty clearing her mind when the sessions ended. She had hoped The Chocola Tree would help—sometimes a good meal can make all the difference—but like her client, she felt ill and had no appetite.

She would never betray the confidence shared with a client, but she wanted to report the man she talked about. It didn't seem right that such behavior was tolerated in a place like Sedona. Selena longed for justice.

The place was packed with a mix of locals and tourists. Many long-time residents swore by the iconic location, believing it was the key to their good health. Most looked vibrant and healthy, although a few others appeared a bit too thin with pasty skin—signs of a vegan diet that wasn't quite balanced to fit their bodies' needs.

A twenty-one-year-old waitress, Malaya, quietly checked in occasionally on Selena and her client but gave them space. She recognized they needed privacy but ensured they had good service, which wasn't always her style.

At times, servers at the restaurant had received bad reviews; one man claimed he had to wait thirty minutes for a table. Another thought his waitress "didn't like him" and went on to say he thought the servers had an "apathetic, borderline hipster attitude," whatever that meant.

Management didn't care because the Chocola Tree was constantly busy, even in the slow season. Malaya knew the locals and always treated them with respect.

Well, most of them.

She loved the bad reviews more than the good ones. They allowed her to be herself because people already didn't know what to expect. She had several jobs in town, another one as a receptionist at a local spa.

Yet, even with both jobs, she had difficulty paying the high rent Sedona landlords demanded. You never knew when a landlord might increase his rent, either, because they were always dreaming about the fortunes they might make if they switched from long-term rentals to short-term Airbnb.

Selena had already finished her Goddess Green Salad. It wasn't much food, but she always had difficulty eating after a session. Later, once she had gone through several rituals to clear the energy, she would be famished.

Her client had barely touched her Broccoli Cheddar Quiche, a local favorite made with pasture-raised eggs and an almond crust.

Selena nodded at the meal and put on a positive voice.

"That meal is too good to waste," she said lightly.

The woman stared at it, her eyes in a trance.

"I'm not hungry."

When Malaya passed next, Selena asked for a to-go container and said, "Well, you know how delicious it is. When you're home later and more relaxed, I want you to eat it — you need to keep your energy up. You're dealing with a lot."

Selena watched the woman as her eyes drifted around the room. She looked like a hunted animal. Too many of her clients had the same look. She wished it were a wide range of reasons for the worried desperation they wore, but it was always the same: men.

As a child in Mexico, she was drawn to the Mayan and Aztec shamanic practices and followed in the footsteps of her female ancestors. Now, at thirty-six, she felt a strong connection to the Earth that kept her grounded.

She had gained power, but in this "man's" world, she knew better than to show it outwardly. Instead, she hid it behind a practical, down-to-earth façade that put people at ease. To others, she seemed only caring and hardworking. She was also ambitious and smart, but knew better than to let men see that side of her.

She didn't crave shaking things up. In fact, she avoided conflict at all costs. Therefore, she tended to give up halfway through projects if they seemed likely to cause others trauma. She kept herself close to the Earth and looked to her ancestors for guidance when she felt anxious or confused.

Malaya returned with the to-go container and the check. Selena paid cash and put her client's food in the container for her.

When the waitress left to get change, Selena said, "You should get some sleep."

The woman nodded meekly and stood to say goodbye.

As the waitress returned, she could hear the woman say, "I can still feel his hands on my neck..."

Selena sat alone for a few minutes after her client left, collecting her thoughts. She thought of treating herself at the restaurant marketplace, which sold organic clothing, beeswax candles, heirloom open-pollinated seeds, and artwork and paintings by local artists.

But after this session, all she wanted to do was go home and relax. Even the Zen-like attitude of the place hadn't helped console her.

When passing through the lobby, she saw Nicola, whom she knew casually from several workshops they had each attended. She was surprised to see an angry look — a fire — in the woman's eyes and even more confused when Nicola confronted her with accusations.

"Are you the one who gave Louis those mushrooms?" demanded Nicola.

Selena was too in control of her emotions to spit out a quick response. Instead, she stared at Nicola for a beat and finally asked. "Why would you ask that?"

Nicola shrugged. "I know you guys are friends, and I also know you sometimes work with psilocybin."

Selena held her ground, but now her eyes flared with anger.

She said, "You throw accusations without knowing any facts. I am not a Shaman, only a Facilitator."

And then, despite her self-control, she added, "Louis is a grown man—he can do what he likes. I shouldn't have to defend myself, but because I know he is your friend, I will tell you, No! I didn't give him any mushrooms."

Nicola nodded, realizing she was out of line.

"I'm sorry," she mumbled. She paused momentarily before asking, "Do you know where he went? He didn't come home last night, and he's not answering his cell."

She sighed. It was a look of desperation she didn't often wear. Nicola added, "I feel like he's in trouble."

Selena held her gaze. "I wish I did."

After Nicola left, Selena thought for a minute. Then she dialed a young woman named Alina because she knew she used mushrooms recreationally—and was also a friend of Louis's.

Chapter Three

Metal

Alina sat in her car at Berry Divine, waiting in the drive-through line to order her Vortex Bowl. On a nearby picnic table, twelve-year-old Kita munched down on a Brazilian Bowl filled with granola and fruit--and extra chocolate drizzle.

Alina was running late for work and drummed her fingers on the steering wheel. She sighed impatiently, then caught the young girl watching her.

Kita grinned, and Alina said, "These guys are pretty fast—I just showed up late."

Kita sat in the shade and enjoyed her bowl. She wasn't in a rush. Two rows of marigolds bracketed the picnic table, and along the wall, someone had planted a row of penstemon; both plants were known to dissuade javalinas. To be safe, the trash and recycling bins were firmly secured in place.

New residents to town often referred to the javalinas as terrorists because of what they did to their gardens and trash cans before they wised up and took action.

Eventually, they joined the debate on whether the creatures were pigs or peccaries, as if this were a new discussion. Sedona students like Kita had been taught the difference long ago. They knew they were peccaries: New World pigs (Tayassuidae), not Old World pigs (Suidae), and had diverged from their common ancestors about 40 million years ago.

When Kita's grandfather stayed with them last, he woke one morning to see upended trash cans and debris spread across the lawn and made plans to purchase several bear traps.

"You can't do that," said her dad. "It's against the law — and you are just as liable to catch a neighbor's dog."

Kita shuddered as she imagined hearing a poor creature — either a dog or a javelina — screaming into the night while the neighbors stood around it debating how to put it out of its misery. And there's nothing comforting about listening to pacifists talk about how they'd kill an animal. Her grandfather had butchered a lot of critters in his hunting days — big and small — and she had no doubt he would just step up and stick the beast in the jugular.

But that's not how they do things in Sedona.

It's also not a good way to make yourself famous. It's almost as bad as getting stranded on a place like Thunder Mountain and requiring a rescue helicopter to come for you. Do that, and the locals will always remember you for that and only that. People always remember the bad shit and forget anything positive you might have done. Even in Sedona, that rule was solid.

At twenty-four, Alina felt the same way. It seemed to her that older people were obsessed with remembering any mistake you ever made. Etch it in stone, for fuck's sake, so it's there for eternity.

What saved the javalinas over the years was that they tasted horrible, no matter how you tried to cook them. She'd heard that even the Apache wouldn't touch them unless they were starving.

Alina moved forward in line and ordered, and Kita observed the side of her car where a friend had painted a fabulous dragon on both sides and the front hood. Alina's windows were down, and Kita asked, "Are you a dragon or just your car?"

Alina grinned. "We both are, I guess. "

Kita nodded. "What kind of dragon?"

Now, Alina's smile broadened even more.

"Well," she began confidently, "if I were a dragon, I'd be the strongest goddamn dragon in the land. I'd be so badass that nobody would mess with me."

Kita admired the young woman's confidence. Not many of her mother's friends were as self-assured and seemingly strong-willed. "Who would mess with you?" asked Kita.

"You'd be surprised," replied Alina with a bit of venom on her tongue, "From my experience, it can be just about anyone."

Then, before Kita could speak, she added, "But it's usually men."

Kita just nodded.

Alina had seen enough of men to know their faults as well as their attributes, and most days, she didn't find their good points balanced out their flaws.

They were taking a while to come out with her Brazilian Bowl, and eventually, Alina added, "Don't get me wrong—I do like men; I just don't have time for their bullshit. Most of my friends are women; you should do the same. When you start to date, make sure you've got some solid sisters by your side."

Again, Kita nodded but kept silent. Her grandmother—a wise woman she much respected—had always said, "Listen twice as much as you speak."

A Red Rock News delivery van pulled up, and a man stepped out, retrieved a bundle of newspapers from the back and stuffed them in an ancient glass-fronted box where people could purchase a copy.

When the guy left, Kita glanced at the headline: Sedona Youth Disappears. She wondered if it might be one of her friends, but upon reading the first paragraph, she saw it was an older guy, Thai-ler, age twenty-nine, who'd been missing for a few days now.

That's a Sedona name if I ever heard one, she thought. I'd bet money he has never been to Thailand, either. More than likely, he was another drifter who tried to make a home here. He probably lived in a shitty van somewhere or surfed from couch to couch.

Women come to Sedona — usually after a divorce — and take yoga, dance and hike. Kita had heard that many classes were 90% female. Men seem to lose their minds here for some reason. Well, some of them, at least. About a quarter of the guys who showed up became self-appointed "teachers," suddenly seeing their calling as gurus or shamans.

Kita had listened to enough of the women around her to know that their ultimate goals were to get grounded, be in the moment, or lose their ego — whatever that meant. Yet these new male shamans went the other way, professing sudden knowledge and insights that they absolutely had to share.

Listening to them go off on the same thing as if it were new was so dull. It bored her to tears. Why couldn't they simply hike and enjoy the place? She would never understand.

A few minutes later, the window slid open, and a man handed Alina a Vortex Bowl. She gave him a twenty, and while she waited for her change, she mixed the blueberries, banana, granola and honey with the purple açaí.

As she was about to take her first bite, her cell phone rang. She didn't recognize the number, but it was local, so she answered.

"Hey, did you sell Louis some mushrooms?"

She paused. "Who is this?"

"This is Selena — you know me," said the voice.

Alina chuckled. "If I knew you, your name would be in my phone."

Selena was losing patience. "Don't screw around. Louis has disappeared, and I'd like to know what happened to him—so please don't mess with me."

Nearby, Kita listened in on the conversation. That's two people missing on the same night, thought Kita. She knew who they were talking about this time. Louis, the author, had spoken to her class a few times, and she liked the guy. He was old but could tell a good story, and he treated the students like adults—or at least not like kids—which was a nice change.

Alina knew him as well. About a year ago, she'd ridden with him to the desert outside Tucson for an ayahuasca ceremony. The next morning, he was still tripping on the ride home and said she had a three-foot-thick halo around her that was made of love. For the next two days, he followed her around like a lost puppy.

He was harmless, although Alina had little patience for infatuations and was ready to tell him to back off if he hit on her. He hadn't. And when they saw each other now, they joked about it.

"Sure," said Alina, a defiant look entering her eyes. "I'll stop messing with you. I will begin by telling you I didn't sell or give him any mushrooms. And I'll also say that Louis is a big boy, and what he does is on him."

The window slid open, and the man handed Alina her change. As she drove off, the last thing Kita heard was Alina asking in a bitter voice, "Are we done here?"

Chapter Four

Water

Kita sat on the bench, watching the dragon car drive away. She didn't know much about dragons besides maybe *Enter the Dragon*, the old Bruce Lee movie her dad had made her watch. It hadn't been all that bad; she'd been taking karate for seven years, since she was five, and having just received her brown belt, she was beginning to feel like a badass.

This confidence allowed her to be patient and observe people. She watched the adults around her the same way she observed her sparring partners, reevaluating situations while understanding the value of not blindly charging forward. Alina had said she would be the strongest of dragons, but Kita already had strength — she was a fighter — so, if she were to be a dragon, she'd want to be something she didn't have now: independent.

At twelve, nobody trusted you to be able to take care of yourself, but she knew she could. When her father had been concerned about a bully in her class who was terrorizing the boys, he'd asked her about it.

"I don't want you to start any trouble," he said, "but I'm curious about what you think about him. If it came down to it, do you think you could take him?"

She'd thought for a minute, evaluating what she knew about the bully and then said, "The boys in my class are stronger, and they roughhouse more, but none of them are fighters. And they wouldn't expect trouble from me, so if I had to, I could drop any of them."

"That's good to hear," he said, "but come to me first if you have any trouble."

Her father was a typical dad, always ready to jump to her defense, but she didn't have the heart to tell him that she was only a few steps away from being able to beat even him if she had to — not that she'd ever fight her dad.

She would never be a damsel who needed rescuing.

She remembered the writer Alina was talking about. He'd come to her classroom to talk about one of his books. The story — the Sirens of Oak Creek — had been interesting, but what she liked more was when the guy had slipped into tales of traveling in Africa… getting chased by a hippo or a crazy honey badger. He would have said, "The trick is to know when to leave the party. When it's time to run!"

Then he'd smile and add, "That's why it's always smart to travel with at least one person who is slow."

When she finished her Berry Divine bowl, she tossed the container in the trash, got on her electric scooter, and headed across town to the Posse Grounds. Once a week, all the Sedona regulars showed up there for a big ecstatic dance, which was always fun to watch — both the dancers and the audience. It was one of those Sedona events that brought out not just the dancers, but all the hippies and freaks.

She took the back way, using Thunder Mountain Road to Sanborn and then Mountain Shadows, rather than 89a, as it cut through town. You could never trust drivers in Sedona. They were always lost, looking at their phone or staring at the damn rocks. When observing Sedona traffic, it didn't take long to realize the drivers were sketchy.

Sometimes, she'd sit on the wall by the Hyatt and watch the vehicles enter the roundabouts at the intersection of 89a and Route 179: About every thirty minutes, someone would go around one of the circles counterclockwise instead of clockwise, often causing an accident — or at least chaos.

She imagined Alina would have said something like, "Fucking dipshits," and she envied her. Nobody wants to hear a twelve-year-old swear, and she was always reprimanded when she tried to throw in a curse word.

Originally, there were no traffic circles, only a T-intersection where 179 joined. Everyone called it "the Y" then — some still did. The town had a contest to rename it after the roundabouts were installed, and her favorite choice was the "y-knot."

A surprising number of tourists acted like they had no concept of how to use a roundabout — or the middle lane in the state highway that ran through town. She wondered if the people only lost their minds while on vacation — staring at their phones while looking for a hotel or restaurant — or if they were that incompetent in their hometowns.

For most of America, firearms were the number one killer of children, be it murder, accidental or suicide, but the drivers visiting Sedona challenged that. Each year, at some point, one of her parents or sisters got tagged by some tourists not looking where he or she was going.

Anyway, she wasn't gonna take any chances, so she stayed on the bike path on her back route, then snaked through a few neighborhoods until she popped out on Soldier's Pass Road and managed to drive the last bit without injury.

When Kita heard the music, she knew she was close to Barbara Antonson Memorial Park, or The Pavilion, as everyone referred to it. Ecstatic Dances were popular in Sedona, with one nearly every day of the week, but the one at the Pavillion was the biggest and drew the most people.

Some folks came just for the crowds.

Most of the other events were held indoors, and everyone who attended danced. However, the Pavilion offered festival-style seating on the grass, and sometimes as many as one hundred and fifty people came to relax, picnic, and watch the dancers.

Kita locked her scooter at the bike rack and walked over. Sedona was the most peaceful town she could imagine, but still, she wasn't about to let some feral hippie steal her only means of transportation.

People were dressed for the occasion. It was one of those events where you could wear any outlandish outfit you wanted. Some had fluorescent paint, ethnic or dayglow clothing, or costumes.

There were also kids and about a dozen dogs running wild through the crowd, too, having their own event. She watched one crazed canine charge into an unsuspecting man and send him sprawling.

Seventy dancers occupied the stage, combining into a sprawling sea of movement. DJ Gabriel BE was mixing the sound —a blissful, world-tribal-house beat—and the air thrummed with pulsating rhythms. Everyone swayed to it in a mesmerizing display.

Gabriel raised his hands in the air just as the music transitioned, and the crowd cheered as one.

Many dancers moved with their eyes closed, lost in their inner worlds. Their bodies undulated and twisted, their arms reaching skyward or sweeping in graceful arcs as if planting their emotions in the air.

They were all unique; some performers executed fluid, serpentine movements, while others engaged in sharp, staccato gestures that punctuated the music's beats. Most danced alone, although a few paired off, combining ecstatic dance with Latin moves.

Kita observed one woman on the stage with numerous tattoos and vibrant purple hair. Her name was Frankie, and she'd once given Kita a tour of an old school bus she was renovating for a big trip across America she was planning. She moved to her own beat and stood out from the dancers around her because of the beautiful smile that accompanied her dance.

There was no question she felt the music.

As Kita walked across the lawn, she smelled marijuana. A fundamental aspect of Ecstatic Dance culture and philosophy is that it's a substance-free event. That may apply to many of the dancers, but the spectators on the lawn made their own rules. Many of the Sedona youths were California Sober, meaning they embraced marijuana and mushrooms and shied away from alcohol.

Being twelve, Kita's one vice was sugar, and the smokers amused her.

A policewoman, Officer Valentina, was there, walking through the crowd. She was in her mid-forties and very competent, but she moved casually and questioned the observers gathered in a relaxed manner.

There were visitors from states where marijuana wasn't legal, and the ones who had purchased some in town suddenly became paranoid when the police officer came by.

That wasn't what Officer Valentina was after, and like Kita, their reaction entertained her more than anything. As Kita watched, she saw the officer holding up a photo of a man in his late twenties, and she knew it was that missing young guy, Thai-ler.

He's probably in Jerome, she thought, smoking weed on someone's couch until they get sick of him.

In the middle of the lawn, Kita spotted a man she knew named Bob. He was holding a baby—Cosmo, his grandson—and she decided to join them and see if she might hold the infant. She could use some baby magic.

49

Bob smiled as she approached and motioned for her to join them on the blanket. As she sat down, she nodded at the baby and put out her hands, and Bob happily handed her over just as Officer Valentina approached them.

"Do you know anything about this young man?" she asked.

Bob nodded. "I've seen him around. Does he live in town?"

The officer gave a slight shoulder shrug.

"Sort of. I'm told he resides in his station wagon, but he's been in Sedona a few months picking up odd jobs—he's been missing a few days now."

Kita snuggled the baby, then dared a question.

"What about that writer guy, Louis?" she asked. "He's missing, too, isn't he?"

A confused expression crossed Officer Valentina's face.

"I hadn't heard about that," she said.

Bob suddenly looked grave. "Louis is missing?"

Kita nodded, and the Officer said, "Well, someone should file a missing person's report—the only one I know about right now is this Thai-ler kid."

Kita sat back and focused on the baby. She was not interested in filing a report. All she knew about either missing person was gossip anyway.

Bob seemed to be of the same persuasion because he held his tongue for a minute, then perked up and asked, "What do you know about the kid?"

Officer Valentina glanced at the stage. "I've heard that he worked a few odd jobs but wasn't that dependable and that he had been messing around in one of the sinkholes in the western canyons out past Bear Mountain."

Bob nodded. "I know Louis liked to hike in that area—do you think they could be connected?"

Officer Valentina shrugged. "Who knows? Do you know anyone who might have any more info on Louis' whereabouts before he disappeared?"

Bob said, "Not really. But, like I said, I know he sometimes wanders out there. He likes Cockscomb Butte for sunsets."

The Officer nodded. "Well, that is in the same vicinity, but that's not much to go on. If you hear anything else, please call the station."

She thanked them and moved on, and Bob said, "I didn't want to drag Louis into a search until I knew more, but it could be Veronica knows something — they're friends, and he takes a weekly private dance class from her.

He glanced at the stage. "You see that woman dancing on the left side of the platform?" he asked.

Kita asked, "The one with all the frizzy hair?"

Bob nodded. "Yeah, that's her — she's Italian, I think about forty, and she is the promoter and organizer of this event. She's also a good friend of Louis' — if anyone knows his whereabouts, it's her."

For a minute, they watched her dance. Her lithe, athletic frame moved with the fluid precision of a seasoned dancer, each step a testament to her dedication to the craft. Her movements commanded attention without demanding it, and Kita found her mesmerizing. She moved with grace and elegance, projecting an aura of serene positivity.

"Wow," said Kita, unsure what to make of her subtle beauty or the peaceful energy she exuded.

"My daughter, Trina, left for the bathroom. When she returns, I'll find Veronica and see if she knows anything."

Suddenly, the song ended, and Veronica walked to D.J Gabriel, who gracefully handed her the microphone. She began speaking; her soft Italian accent instantly caught everyone's attention, and even those in the audience became silent.

Bob looked at Kita. "We're gonna have to wait a while — this is the wind-down, and it may be a half-hour before she's free."

"That's okay," said Kita, "I gotta run."

The sun was setting, the temperatures were dropping, and she had to go. She suddenly remembered something Louis had told her class, which made her feel she might know where he had gone.

Just then, Trina returned, and Kita stood and handed the baby to her mother.

Trina sat on the blanket, listening to Veronica's message of peace and love. Suddenly, Cosmo's face took on a look of discomfort.

A minute later, Trina said, "We should head to the car. This little guy needs a diaper change."

"Fine," said Bob. "I'm starving anyway—feel like some sushi?"

Trina nodded as she helped Bob pack up their belongings.

Thunder Mountain

Chapter Five

Wood

Cosmo slept in his car seat, which had been attached to a chair inside Hiro's Sushi & Japanese Kitchen. Bob and Trina sat next to him and scanned the menu. Outside, a fiery sunset was shouting out the last colors of the day.

At the table beside them, an older, white-haired woman sipped her miso soup while waiting for a spider roll.

On the wall, a television showed the local news, and currently, a story about the missing youth was running. The older woman watched it with a gleeful look of satisfaction.

Cosmo's grandfather, Bob, was retired but had spent much of his life working as a Rolfer. He was an energy guy and very sensitive — and susceptible — to the forces around him. Often, he would drive to Flagstaff to visit a few groves of trees — Douglas firs and Ponderosa pines — where he had befriended several trees. There, he would sit patiently, hands on the trees, and communicate and share.

Even before Cosmo was born, Bob had an interesting relationship with his grandson, who had been exchanging thoughts since he was in the womb.

Behind a counter, Hiro, an experienced sushi chef, or *Itamae*, worked on preparing the spider roll while the television blared above him. The story about the missing young man had been going on for a few days. And through gossip, he'd also heard about a lost writer now. Being a sushi chef was like being a bartender, and you listened to all sorts of things because people forgot about you while you worked and didn't seem to realize you could hear everything.

Neither story surprised him. He did know the writer, a regular, and hoped he was okay.

Sedona seemed to bring out the extremes in people, and being surrounded by thousands of square miles of high desert left opportunities for people to get lost, physically and mentally.

Hiro was born in Japan but grew up in America. He didn't know his birth country, but that didn't stop its influence, especially with grandparents and parents constantly reminding him. He had noticed an abnormally high number of women here, but it had taken his grandmother, who based everything on the Japanese zodiac system, to tune him into the fact that there were also a lot of dragons in town.

He didn't really believe in the Japanese zodiac system, which was close to Chinese astrology, but that didn't stop certain observations that constantly backed it up. There were twelve signs: rat, ox, tiger, rabbit, dragon, horse, snake, goat, monkey, rooster, dog and pig.

His grandmother had told him Sedona's intense natural energy attracted dragons, and he sensed that for himself. For instance, the white-haired woman sitting at the table was a regular who had celebrated her birthday last month. He knew she was born in 1952, which made her a dragon—a fire dragon, to be exact.

The baby sleeping in the car seat was about six months old, making it a dragon also because this was the year of the dragon. And the missing writer was about to turn sixty, making him a dragon, too. Whether you were talking about the Chinese or

Japanese systems, both had characters that repeated every twelve years. So, going back in time, dragons would have been born in 1952, 1964, 1976, 1988, 2000, and 2012.

Hiro knew the old woman's birth year because Camille was a regular and usually sat at the bar and talked to him. Lately, she had been obsessed with getting several young men arrested because they continuously snuck onto her property in the western canyons. There was a sinkhole on it that attracted them, and they refused to give up on their efforts.

Here, a small shaft led underground, and at night, some of these kids would tiptoe onto her land with small shovels and try to dig down into the chute, hoping it might open into a cavern.

There were massive aquifers under Sedona, and these young men hoped they might immerse themselves in one and discover a new cave system. The local authorities didn't approve of this because it was dangerous, and one could get killed doing such explorations in numerous ways. They might get trapped underground, or they just might find a cave and drop into it, and who knows how far that plunge might be.

"Dragons," his grandmother would say, "are too powerful and often come with trouble." This always made Hiro uncomfortable because he was born in 1976, making him a dragon himself.

They weren't all the same, though. There were five variations: wood, fire, earth, metal and water, and they each came with different attributes.

At first, he didn't believe any of it and scoffed at the importance his family put into the symbols, but his observations increasingly fit the bill. Imagination? Maybe. Coincidence? Probably.

Yet he still found the dragons he encountered in Sedona, many times sitting before him, all acted as they should according to the system—and there did seem to be a high percentage of dragons in this town. His grandparents had noticed it, and because he was a dragon, they decided it was why he was meant to live in Sedona.

They constantly reminded him of what to expect from each dragon as if it would protect him. This catalogue of things to worry about was exhausting, and he wished figuring out people was more straightforward.

His grandmother would run through the list, saying, "Wood dragons are introverted and dedicated to their work, Fire dragons are highly adaptable and good at seizing opportunities, Earth dragons are smart and ambitious, and so on..."

They also based his sign on who to befriend and who to avoid because, depending on the year you were born, you might be an entirely different type of dragon, snake, pig, or whatever sign you were born to. It was complicated.

"Dragons don't get along with domestic animals, like the ox, horse and goat, but they are fine with the pig for some reason. That was most likely a good thing for the baby before him, a wood dragon, because his grandfather was a fire pig, which meant he had attributes that might help the boy. Fire pigs were known for their loyalty, warmth, and nurturing nature.

His grandfather was more taciturn and rarely talked about it, but he would occasionally say, "Avoid dogs at all costs," and Hiro knew he was talking about people born in the year of the dog, not the kind of animals some kept as pets.

"Dragons should not trust dogs," was all the old man would say, as if that were enough."

This young man, who had disappeared, was a dog. Was that a coincidence? He wondered. It seemed there were a lot of coincidences in this strange town.

When Hiro had finished the spider roll, he gave it to a server, who brought it out to Camille. She smiled a thank you, placed a napkin on her lap, and picked up a piece of sushi with her chopsticks.

She was about to take her first bite when she glanced over and saw Cosmo had woken.

His grandfather and mother were in a conversation, but he didn't look at them. Instead, the baby stared at Camille with an intensity that unnerved her.

She wanted to look away, but couldn't. All the hair on her neck and the backs of her forearms stood on end. She felt time slow down to a crawl around her.

The news had circled back to missing Thai-ler, and for a moment, the baby moved his attention to the television screen before sliding his eyes back to Camille.

She set down the sushi.

Cosmo continued to look intently at her. It was more of a glare that appeared unnatural coming from an innocent baby.

Suddenly, Camille felt like she was about to get sick.

Moments before, she'd been famished; now, she knew if she even tried to eat, she would vomit.

She stood and rushed to the door. The server gave her a questioning look but let her pass. Soon, her truck could be seen backing up and speeding out of the parking lot, leaving a cloud of dust in its wake.

The server looked at Hiro and said, "She left without paying and didn't even touch the roll."

He knew she would eventually return and pay for her meal, but said nothing. Instead, he nodded to the server and thought, "Fucking dragons."

Bob looked down and saw Cosmo's eyes gazing at the parking lot. He could tell, or felt, something significant had happened, but didn't know what.

The news anchor still rambled on about missing Thai-ler.

Bob leaned over and looked into Cosmo's eyes. After a second, the baby raised his hand and pointed west.

"Oh my," said Bob, thinking the gesture reminded him of Babe Ruth calling his shot in game three of the 1932 World Series when he pointed and then hit a home run over the center field.

"What's going on?" asked Trina.

Bob stared at the baby for about thirty seconds, observing the hand still pointing west. Then he said, "I think we're gonna pack up and go for a drive."

"Where?" asked Trina, confused.

Bob shrugged. "West."

Louis lay dreaming in a crevice between two rocks where he had fallen the night before. He had smashed his forehead, and a trickle of blood had flowed from the injury and matted into his hair.

In the dream, a large animal had been snuggling against him, affectionately rubbing its muzzle into his neck. He had felt the warmth of its breath and the slight tickle of the whiskers against his skin. The beast had lain beside him, and he remembered its warmth in the night.

At least, that's what the dream had been of.

Although he couldn't see the animal in the dream, he felt no fear. Its purring and body warmth had been comforting.

Slowly, he roused himself, waking from a slumber that had felt like death. He'd been unconscious the entire day after hitting his head and had no idea where he was or how he'd gotten outside.

When he finally opened his eyes, he saw a mountain lion perched on one of the rocks by his side. It was about five feet away. The full moon had risen, and the big cat looked mythical in its glow. The luminescent yellow eyes were surrounded by black eyelid skin, which gave the appearance of eyeliner.

Louis couldn't move; he was still dazed, but he watched the animal for a minute, unsure of what to do. The cat ignored him until he sniffed, and then their eyes locked.

As he came around and the dream state left him, he was just beginning to be fearful of the cat when the "crack" of a stick caught both of their attention.

To their right, Kita came into view.

The cat roared and then bounded out of sight.
Kita watched it, smiling and unafraid.

At the Ecstatic Dance, Kita remembered when the writer, Louis, told the class that of all the places on the planet, the one most sacred to him was the top of Cockscomb Butte.

She hadn't said anything to Officer Valentina or Bob because she'd felt it was a wild hunch, even though they'd each mentioned Cockscomb. Yet, as she drove there, she slowly gained confidence that if Louis had been in that area, in trouble or not, that's most likely where he would have gone.

She had hopped on her scooter and retraced her earlier journey back to Dry Creek Road, where she hoped she had enough charge to get into the western canyons and to the trailhead for Cockscomb Butte.

She ignored the fact that she would most likely not have enough power to get all the way home, leaving her stranded.

She knew she'd find a way.

The sun had set, and the full moon glowed above her.

When she reached the trailhead, she hid the scooter in the bushes because there was no bike rack. Then she began following the trail, which went for about a mile before reaching the foot of the butte.

Thankfully, because of the rising moon, she didn't need a flashlight. In the distance, she heard some coyotes singing to the moon—and once, an owl hooted.

Halfway there, she began questioning whether Louis might be there at all. She heard her father's voice stating, "This is a fool's journey."

She followed the rugged trail up the side of the butte and then onto its flat top. Under the soft glow, she had searched unsuccessfully and was about to depart for the parking lot when she saw the big cat.

Her heart had stopped for a second, and then it beat five times as fast as normal when the big cat roared defiantly.

How beautiful, she thought. Thankfully, it had fled after seeing her, and by the time she reached Louis' side, she felt they were alone.

Louis looked dazed and only fully came to when she pulled out her phone and suggested calling for help. He put his hand on her cell phone to prevent her from dialing. Kita respected that he didn't want to be "famous" through a public rescue and took his elbow and helped him along.

"I appreciate the offer," he said, "but there's no way I'm getting rescued up here. I think I can walk fine."

He stood on shaky legs but seemed otherwise fine as they crossed the small plateau to the place that allowed them to descend to the trail.

On the way down, his feet slipped from under him a few times on the loose scree. The trail leveled out when they made it off the side of the butte, which was good because his energy was beginning to fade.

When they reached the trailhead parking lot, Kita began questioning the logic behind not calling for help. She doubted her scooter had the power to get back to town, and she wasn't sure if Louis even had the energy to stand behind her while they drove the seven miles.

She had retrieved the scooter from the brush, set it on the pavement, and asked Louis to stand behind her.

"Do you think you can do it?" she asked.

He nodded distantly and was about to step on the back of the scooter when Bob drove his BMW into the parking lot and pulled up next to them.

"Cosmo thought you might need a lift," he said with a grin.

Rabbit and Bread Loaf

Robert Louis DeMayo

WEDNESDAY

Chapter Six

Water

*C*amille thought a massage was just what she needed. And not just any massage… she requested a ninety-minute sandalwood body treatment with hot stones and deep tissue.

She had been coming to Uptown Massage for years, first to their place on Jordan Road and then to West Sedona after their former landlord tripled their rent.

Usually, she only requested sixty minutes and no deep tissue. She was a cowgirl and considered herself tough, and massages were indulgences that felt too extravagant. Her husband would have teased her, then told her to enjoy it, but he was long gone, dead from a heart attack ten years ago.

She had never declared his death; she put him in the ground on their property in a big hole she dug with their little excavator. It was what he wanted: no funeral, no wake, and no government involvement. He was an old timer—never liked the new Sedona that emerged out of the seventies—and cursed the tourists as their numbers grew over the years.

He'd called the John Deere mini-excavator, "Charlie," and a week before he died, he'd given her a serious stare and said, "Better get Charlie fired up for a little work."

She still cashed his social security checks; something she had been warned would one day catch up with her, but she didn't care. She'd be dead soon enough anyway.

It was an act of defiance that she knew he would have liked. She missed sitting on the porch with him, watching the sun descend behind Mingus Mountain to the west. During those final moments of blessed light, the panorama of limestone cliffs surrounding their ranch in the western canyons would glow a profound mix of red, orange and pink, making words seem useless and insufficient.

Her husband had been a man of few words anyway. He never spoke during sunset, but after that, in the thickening darkness, he sometimes came alive for a few minutes while he shared his day. In the years since his passing, she still watched the sun dip behind Mingus and often yearned for those few clips of his day that he dished out in the darkness.

"I mended that broken fence down by Bradshaw draw…"

"Found that missing calf having a little nap by the tank…"

"I think we might need more hardwood for the winter… "

Ten years gone now, she thought, and all I have of him are a few photos and those clips of conversation.

Now, with new dramas unfolding, she booked a massage and hoped it might help soothe things.

"You could use a break," she imagined him saying.

He talked to her often these days.

Malaya greeted her when she entered Uptown Massage. After Chocola Tree, this was her second job, and she thought the slower pace balanced things out. And she made a reasonable hourly wage, so she didn't rely on tips.

It was easy, too. After she checked in the guests and put them in a room waiting for their therapists, there wasn't much to do other than maybe bring a bundle to the laundrymat.

Robert Louis DeMayo

People leaving the massage table rarely complained, which was also nice. She'd even been mentioned positively in a few reviews, which she found amusing.

Malaya noticed Camille seemed jittery, not quite herself, when she greeted her at the door.

"Would you like some water?" she asked.

Camille shrugged and lifted her metal water flask.

"Thanks," she said, "I got that covered."

Malaya nodded; Camille had always been too tough to let anyone coddle her. She liked these strong, older Arizona women. The desert here had touched them — hardened them — she supposed.

Where can I get some of that strength? she pondered. Most people only saw white hair and wrinkles when they looked at Camille, but Malaya thought she was admirable.

The last time she came in, she was early, and the two sat outside on the bench so as not to bother the clients currently getting massaged. On that visit, it was Malaya who had been disturbed.

The night before, she'd had a date with a boy that had gone wrong because he'd been aggressive while kissing her goodnight. "I told him to stop," she'd said, "but he wouldn't."

Camille had held her tongue for a minute, letting Malaya finish, then asked, "What'd you do?"

Malaya sighed. "Well, luckily, we were in the restaurant parking lot. I smacked him in the head, and when he backed off, I quickly jumped out of his station wagon. People were around us, so he didn't even leave the car; he just drove away."

"Good girl," nodded Camille. "Guys like that need to have their balls cut off."

Today, she escorted the older woman to her assigned room and said, "Alina will be your therapist today. I see you've booked a ninety-minute Sandalwood massage with deep tissue."

"I sure did," replied Camille, trying to sound upbeat.

"Good for you," said Malaya. I hope you enjoy it. Please get undressed and lie face down on the table, and Alina will be right in."

Soon, Alina entered and greeted Camille. After exchanging pleasantries, they talked for a few minutes about the treatment.

"Anything new going on with your body?" asked Alina, noticing her tense frame as she lay before her, her body refusing to relax into the table like it was a bed of coals.

Camille, eyes closed, her head held in a soft face cradle, mumbled, "Well, I have been a little stressed lately."

Alina grinned. "We can take care of that."

Over the next ninety minutes, Alina worked out the knots and tension in the old woman's muscles. Soft music played throughout the spa, and a fountain in the corner tinkled a soothing song. The hot stones did their trick.

Outside the room, Camille could faintly hear voices. She recognized the owner, Diana, as she checked in with Malaya, and together, they reviewed the day's schedule. Most of it was muffled except when they passed close to the door.

Camille tried her best to think about nothing, but images kept flashing before her mind's eye. A dark night lit horizontally by a moon peaking over the horizon... a truck headlight sweeping the ground... and a voice pleading for help.

She clamped her eyes tighter and forgot where she was for a few seconds until Alina said, "Wow, you do have some tension in your shoulders..."

The older woman grunted.

Alina added, "The sandalwood should help—it reduces inflammation and soothes aches."

Again, Camille mumbled an affirmative.

It was enough of a reply for Alina. She didn't need to fill the massage with conversation, but instead wanted to give Camille the chance to talk about her pain if she was ready—clearly, the woman was dealing with something because her body was as tense as a piano string. Or, in her case, barbed wire.

She knew Camille was acquainted with the young man who had disappeared. It was common knowledge that he'd been trespassing on her property and being a nuisance. She had also let it be known that she didn't think much of the kid.

It didn't surprise her as she knew Thai-ler casually. He was five years older than Alina and not bad looking, but he was definitely the type of guy she avoided. You didn't have to be an expert on men to know he was trouble, and since his disappearance, she'd heard a few rumors about him that made her glad she'd always kept her distance. Could there be other reasons that Camille was so tense? She wondered.

Alina was much younger than Camille, but knew people came for massages to relax their minds as much as their bodies. Sometimes, clients talked straight through the entire treatment, unloading their baggage like they'd gone to a psychiatrist.

That could get heavy, but the fountains and soft music usually mixed with the hot stones and soothed it all away. You just had to give the clients a chance now and then to put it out there.

Alina asked, "Anything new in your life that's got you so tense?"

Camille's reply was tight-lipped. "Nope."

And then she added, "No, really," like she was trying to convince Alina that she was okay. She didn't buy it.

Outside the room, Malaya sat in a chair in the lobby, checking her cell phone messages. Diana had run to the bank, and the next massages didn't begin for an hour, so those people had yet to check in.

She was only a few feet from the room where Alina worked on Camille, and she had to be quiet, so her phone was on silent, but the morning sun was streaming in the window, and right now, this was the best seat in the house.

She heard Alina ask about the old woman's stress and her muffled replies. A few minutes later, Alina left the room after telling Camille to take her time and to let the massage sink in before getting off the table.

Many of the clients at Uptown Massage were treated like family. The spa was one of the few in town not attached to a big, fancy hotel and, over the years, had helped many residents deal with anything from a torn muscle to a broken heart from divorce. It was a local place.

Before Alina left, she whispered in Camille's ear, "Are you sure you're okay, honey? Did anything happen you'd like to talk about?"

Camille only grunted again, and Alina left.

On the chair outside the room, Malaya winked at Alina as she left to use the bathroom before her client emerged from the room. Malaya returned to her phone and was surprised when she heard Camille whisper to herself in the room.

She only said five words: "I did a bad thing."

Gunsight rock

Chapter Seven

Fire

Nicola woke from another bad dream. It was worse than the other, filled with swirling fear and a dark panic. But this time, she knew Louis was okay. She was staying with an astrologer friend, Carrie, and they'd been notified through the Sedona grapevine within an hour of Bob and Cosmo picking him up.

Bob had driven Louis home and, on the way, contacted his doctor. Luckily, Doctor Jason was also a friend, and he was waiting in Louis' driveway when they pulled in. Louis had a nasty gouge on his forehead, but it required no stitches, and he wasn't concussed.

By ten o'clock, Doctor Jason pronounced him fit to go to bed.

"Call the office in the morning," he said as he left, "and let Angie know you're still doing fine." Then he grinned and added, "And no more vision quests for a few weeks."

Louis grunted an affirmative, and the doc walked away, shaking his head.

So why do I still have this terrible feeling? Nicola asked herself when she first woke up. Something bad was happening right now; she could sense it. She paced her friend's kitchen in the pre-dawn light, hoping not to wake her.

Not one to sit around thinking about what to do, she was dressed and heading for the western canyons by 8:00 am. For Nicola, it seemed too much of a coincidence that Louis and that young kid, Thai-ler, disappeared on the same night.

Although nobody knew where Thai-ler was before he stopped showing up for work, she had been told he was one of the people digging into a sinkhole near Bear Mountain. And that wasn't far at all from Cockscomb Butte.

She wanted to ask Louis questions, but felt it was best to let him sleep for a while. She thought about asking Jenn at Hot Yoga if she had heard any new gossip, but she didn't have the patience to sit through a class.

The dream had left a restlessness in her.

She tightened her boots at the Cockscomb parking lot and took a small backpack with a water bottle and a few oranges she'd snagged at Carrie's.

The approach to the butte was straightforward. The trail wound through a forest of pinion pines and shaggy bark juniper, covering about a mile on fairly level ground. The area only got snow a few times a year, and the ground never froze, but it was still winter, with more browns and yellows and no bright green.

The trail was bracketed by clusters of prickly pear cactus or manzanita bushes, neither of which are fun to move through. Luckily, the path was well-maintained and used daily by mountain bikers.

Once she reached the butte, the bike trail continued, skirting around it. There was no regulated trail going up the butte. The forest service didn't want people up there, and if you got stuck and needed to be rescued, it'd be on your dime, which was another reason Louis had been adamant about not wanting to be rescued up there.

But all the locals knew the way, and after the first one hundred feet, where the forest service had obscured the trail, you could easily see how everyone went. It slowly zig-zagged up the butte's eastern side before ascending to the southern end.

She walked around the top for an hour, trying to find a clue or maybe sense something more, but failed. She sat heavily and stared over the land as it stretched west to Mingus Mountain and Sycamore Canyon. She ate one of her oranges.

The high desert up here was breathtaking, and she regretted doing this hike with such blinders on. Nicola relaxed for ten minutes, breathing steadily, and then she snuck a small hit off her pipe before she descended.

She had a second water bottle in the car, which she tapped into after sitting down. So, Cockscomb didn't have any answers, she thought. Now, on to the sinkhole.

She had asked around and learned a few things: The Verde Valley has seven sinkholes. Some have cool names, like the Devil's Kitchen or the Devil's Dining Room. They are also different sizes, with the largest being Red Canyon, 225 feet wide and 100 feet deep. They are formed due to the collapse of rocks into cavernous Redwall Limestone that lies 600 feet below the surface. Massive aquifers under this area fill some of the empty spaces. There's a concern that contaminated groundwater or unregulated septic leakage could find a way into the aquifers and ruin the town's drinking water.

Even though everyone said there was a sinkhole nearby, there might not have been. What was on Camille's property might have been a vent or fumarole. Here, air rushed out of the earth, coming from a subterranean chamber or through underground paths before exiting elsewhere.

The young men had been digging into it for a few months, showing up in gortex jackets, with shovels and battery-powered lamps, before she stopped them. According to

Camille, they were all hippies, and it had yet to be explored by a scientist.

Camille employed a gruff man in his forties named Lars to help with odd chores and physical work. These days, he guarded the site day and night.

It was only a half-mile away from Nicola now, so she drove that way, slowing a little when the pavement ended and the road turned to fine red dust.

She put her car in park when she saw the guy standing by the entrance to Camille's ranch, poised like a Pitbull. She figured she would ask him a few questions, but no sooner had she stepped out of the car when he held up his hand.

"That's far enough, lady," said Lars with a tone that irked Nicola. From twenty feet away, she could tell he was a mean prick.

"Can I ask you something?" she said.

He snapped back. "No, you can't — get the fuck out of here."

She held her ground. "It's about that missing kid?"

He scowled and said, "Of course it is. That fucking kid has been nothing but trouble. It's why we sealed up the hole last week. I'm sick of it — so is Camille — so git! Go away."

Not one to retreat, Nicola took a half step forward, but he moved his shirt aside to show a large pistol.

He said, "I might not shoot you, but I'll put a few holes in your car if you don't leave."

He glared at her as he pulled out the gun. "Might do it anyway — you're trespassing."

Nicola scoffed. "Chill out, asshole. I'm leaving."

Javalinas

Chapter Eight

Earth

Selena sat near the window in the Dragon's Den, looking at the parking lot while she sipped her morning tea. A faint whisp of incense floated through the store. She'd been working at the boutique for six months and had grown accustomed to being surrounded by crystals, chimes and other metaphysical items, and she enjoyed the fact that coming to work relaxed her.

They also always played good music.

The owner, a busy guy named Ryan, was always making something happen at the Den or one of his other businesses. He owned a tour company, managed a food truck and hosted a few non-profit community events. She forgave him for his hectic pace because he'd show up at some ecstatic dances in town, and Selena had seen that he could dance.

She thought that anyone with rhythm who is willing to dance with others deserves a chance in this life.

On the shelf, she glanced at *The Sirens of Oak Creek*, a novel by Louis, the guy who'd been knocked out while doing his version of a walkabout. Louis was a good friend of hers, but she didn't approve of some of his drug use.

She thought of checking in on him, but she didn't want to disturb him if he was recovering. Then again, it was noon; knowing him, he'd be up and running by now regardless of yesterday. He hated lying around in bed. On a Wednesday in the off-season, she could just stop by on her lunch break.

She had no reason to stay at work. Besides the few tourists finishing their breakfast at Café Jose, there wouldn't be many potential customers on the sidewalk.

She took out her cell and looked up Nicola's Facebook page, where she had a few events listed. On the bottom of one was her cell number for those wanting to book. She dialed it and was relieved when Nicola answered.

"Hello friend," she said, "what can I do for you?"

"Good morning," said Selena, a bit awkwardly. "I heard they found Louis—I guess I'm making sure he is okay."

"Well, I'm with him right now, on our way to Tortas del Fuego for lunch. Care to meet us?"

Selena knew Knox would be in soon for her shift, and they didn't need two people staffing the store when the town was so slow, so she said, "Sure thing, I can be there in about twenty."

Earlier, Nicola had expected to find Louis in bed with an ice pack, but instead, he was in the kitchen, washing dishes while his coffee machine brewed up an espresso shot.

"What are you doing up?" she had asked through the screen when she peered inside and saw him. "You should be in bed."

"Ah, I couldn't sleep," he said. Louis was wearing L.L. Bean shorts, black boots and a grey T-shirt. Outwardly, he looked ready to go on another hike, but he was moving slowly and didn't seem one hundred percent yet.

At least, that's how Nicola perceived him.

"Why don't you let me make the coffee?" she asked, subtly moving him to a stuffed chair. He nodded and looked disoriented.

"I did get about four hours of sleep, but my brain just wakes up in the morning. It does no good trying to sleep after that—I just lay there thinking," said Louis.

She raised a motherly eyebrow, and he shrugged.

"Don't worry, I'll get a nap in later."

Nicola still wanted to ask Louis a few questions, but saw the confused look in his eyes. Instead, she took the shot off the machine, poured it into a coffee cup, and added a squirt of honey. "Here you go, luv," she said with a smile.

He looked flattered that she remembered how he took it.

She grinned. She had questions she wanted to ask him; however, he needed to be stable first. That dark feeling still nagged at her, but she had no choice. She glanced at the kitchen and asked, "Can I make you anything else? Some toast?"

Now, Louis came around. "I want a whole breakfast. I haven't eaten for almost two days, and my fridge is empty."

Nicola grabbed his jacket and handed it to him.

"That's a problem I can fix," she said. "I'm taking you to lunch—we're getting shrimp tacos."

Selena greeted the hostess and chatted in Spanish as they walked to the table where Nicola and Louis were already seated. The new dining room at the restaurant had been a hit, and it was full of people.

In the next booth, Kita sat with her mother, having lunch.

Louis had a small bandage on his forehead, but a more extensive area had already started to bruise and yellow. He seemed distracted, and Selena could see that he wasn't entirely back to normal.

Nicola slid over and said, "You can sit next to me—we'll give Quasimodo some breathing room." She had tried to joke, but her eyes were serious.

Something in Nicola's expression spoke of a restlessness in her that Selena couldn't quite understand, as Louis seemed like there was no permanent damage, and with a bit of rest, he'd be fine.

She cleared it up when she asked, "Do you know anything about that missing kid, Thai-ler? They still haven't found him, and it bothers me."

Selena stared at her for a minute. Nicola was twelve years older than her, and she had always appeared sure and confident the few times they'd met before—but that was missing now. In its place was a jitteriness, like a nagging voice in the background.

But why was she so worried about Thai-ler? She didn't think they knew each other. And why did she also feel it was somehow connected to Louis? That was the problem with energy workers, thought Selena. They were always susceptible to the forces around them, whether they liked it or not.

The waiter brought chips and salsa, and Louis attacked them voraciously.

The dining room at Tortas had several televisions over the bar, one of which flashed the ongoing narrative about the missing kid. Nearby, Kita watched the same story while her mom replied to messages on her cell phone. Behind her, she listened to the two women talking to Louis.

Selena sadly chuckled at the thought that nobody had even noticed Louis' disappearance. It wasn't a surprise, as Louis and his friends had not wanted anyone to know.

As she watched Louis down another chip loaded with salsa, she wondered if he might have helpful information.

"What do you remember about your ordeal?" asked Selena, who knew she was on the right track by the relaxed expression that suddenly came over Nicola's face.

Kita had also wondered the same thing, and her ears perked up as she eavesdropped.

Louis shrugged and tried to smile. "Surprisingly little—it's like my mind has gone blank."

Nicola said, "Officer Valentina called him to say they found his Buick out on Bradshaw Hill."

The waiter brought a dish of three shrimp tacos and couldn't decide who to set it in front of, but Nicola laughed and nodded at Louis.

"Give him the plate," she said, "or I believe he might fight us for it."

The waiter set it down and said, "The rest will be out in just a minute."

Louis took a huge bite and then, with a full mouth, said, "Thank you – I can't believe how hungry I am – and I could use a hand picking up my car later if either of you are free."

Selena grimaced. "I shouldn't take my car that far down a dirt road – it's got front-end issues."

Nicola shrugged. "My rig can handle it."

Selena waited a minute before pressing Louis again.

"Nothing?" she asked. "Do you remember leaving your car? Or driving out into that area?"

Louis thought about the night and eventually said, "I remember driving by the Stupa parking lot… that's it."

Nicola looked frustrated but didn't say anything.

Selena stared at Louis for a solid moment before speaking.

"I think the trauma has currently buried those memories," she said, "would you be willing to work with me for a few minutes to see if I can help you remember?"

One taco was gone as Louis tore into a second. The waiter returned and set two more plates in front of the ladies. Louis took another big bite and said, "Happy to, although I don't know what good it will do to know what crazy shit I was up to out there – I pretty much just stumbled around. Heck, I don't even know how I ended up on Cockscomb."

Selena gave Nicola a slight nod and said, "You never know; I think it would be helpful."

"Okay," replied Louis, "what do I do?"

Selena shook her head. "Not here. Eat your tacos, and after, we will find a quiet place up by the Stupa."

When Louis left for the bathroom, Selena said to Nicola, "You think he saw something that night, don't you?"

Nicola shrugged. "It was the same area, and my gut feeling is that he might have."

Kita listened to their conversation and wondered why they weren't heading there. Everyone knew the kid had been messing with that sinkhole not too far from Cockscomb — what were they waiting for? She often marveled when listening to adults at how they could talk and talk without ever doing anything.

Twenty minutes later, Selena and Louis sat in the shade of a juniper, a stone's throw from the stupa. Tibetan prayer flags snapped in the wind, accompanied by the sound of a few chimes hidden in the brush. A few people offered prayers and thanks and walked the path around the stupa, but otherwise, the place was empty.

Selena had Louis sit comfortably under the tree, and while he adjusted, she lit some sage and set it in a small shell she drew from her purse.

She had him close his eyes and breathe deeply.

She said, "I want you to take twenty deep breaths and clear your mind." As he did, she lightly shook a rattle to create a low rumbling sound, not unlike distant thunder.

Now and then, she encouraged him with calm, evenly paced words...

"Forget everything else in the world... think only of the wind in the tree branches or birdsong."

Slowly, Louis unwound. His facial muscles relaxed. His shoulders dropped, and his breathing became regular.

Selena picked up the shell with the burning sage and, using a ceremonial prayer fan of several macaw feathers, fanned the smoke over Louis.

"Now," she began, "I want you to imagine yourself sitting on the hood of your Buick looking over the western canyons.

It's nighttime, but the stars are lighting up everything — as is the rising moon."

She waited a minute before asking, "Can you see the canyons lit up in starlight?"

Louis nodded and spoke from a distance. "I can."

"Okay," said Selena while nodding to herself.

Then, "Now I want you to start walking — where are you going?"

Louis' eyebrows crunched for a minute before he said, "I'm walking east — in the direction of the singing coyotes."

Over the next ten minutes, she followed him through his wanderings. A lot didn't make sense to her, and she wondered if it did to Louis, but none of it seemed connected to a missing person.

Then Louis began describing a truck parked with its lights suspended over what looked like a fresh grave.

"I don't feel comfortable here," said Louis. "There's something bad going on."

"What else can you tell me about the truck?" asked Selena.

Louis was silent for a minute and then said, "It's a white truck, but the highs are on. I can't see anything else."

Selena took a slow breath, then asked, "And what else? Are you alone?"

Louis, eyes still shut, moved his head like he was looking around. "There is someone here. I heard the words, 'Serves you right.'"

Short, choppy breaths issued from Louis. He was back at that moment, afraid and confused. Selena dared to ask one more question before she pulled him back.

"Can you tell me anything else about the speaker?"

After a minute, Louis added, "She's female."

Chapter Nine

Metal

Alina sat at an outside table at Vino de Sedona, a popular wine bistro in west Sedona. It was open mike night, and currently, an acoustic group called the Blue Agave Trio was belting out a lively folk tune. The evening had just begun, with a sky full of rippled clouds reflecting the red glow of an ongoing sunset.

Through the door, she saw Malaya, whom she knew from Uptown Massage, and waved her over.

Once seated, the two listened to the music for a while, but when there was a quiet moment between songs, Malaya leaned over and asked, "What did you think of Camilla today? She seemed like something was bothering her."

Alina nodded. "I felt the same way — she seemed off."

A new act came forward — two members of a larger group called Javalina Highway — and they listened to their first song as it floated over the courtyard.

When the waitress came by, they decided to splurge and ordered a bottle of Vino del Barrio Red from the nearby Page Spring Cellars. The waitress, new to town, smiled and said, "That's a great choice — it blends a zinfandel, syrah, cab and a petite sirah."

Both women smiled patiently and then at the same time said, "We know." They grinned at each other as the waitress walked off.

A few minutes later, the band took a break, announcing there would be a slight pause in the entertainment.

Eventually, Alina said, "I suppose having those young men trespassing on her property every night might have worn her down—that's got to be unnerving."

Malaya nodded. "Yeah, that's true. But she had her guy fill in the sinkhole a few days ago, so that can't be it. She should be relaxed at this point."

"Well, there's also missing Thai-ler," added Alina. "He was on her property, and they say he spent a lot of time in that area."

"I know he parked his station wagon at the Doe Mesa trailhead lot from time to time—slept there too when digging at the sinkhole, "said Malaya, "but it wasn't there when he went missing."

Alina shrugged. "Maybe he just split—I know there are a lot of people in this town, mostly women, who would be glad to see him gone."

Malaya stared at her friend for a beat, then said, "I wouldn't cry if I never saw him again." She thought of their one date, when he'd tried to force himself on her in the parking lot of Pizza Picasso. She also remembered Selena talking to a client at The Chocola Tree, and how the woman had said a man had tried to choke her—she felt certain it was the same guy.

"When I heard he was one of the boys digging into that sinkhole, I hoped he'd get stuck down there—or maybe fall to his death into some subterranean cavern."

Alina's face became serious. "You had an encounter with him, too? Wow, that guy got around. What a fuckin' dog."

The two sat there quietly for a minute until Alina asked, "And when was the last time anyone saw that little punk?"

Malaya shrugged. "Thai-ler? I believe it was the night before Camille had the sinkhole filled in. Maybe he figured that was a sign to leave town."

The waitress returned, and Alina went through the motions of tasting the wine and approving the bottle before she filled both glasses.

A short while later, Officer Valentina walked through the courtyard, and they flagged her over. She was off duty, wearing civilian clothes; her hair was down, and she wore a flowery dress, which showed off a completely different side of her.

They flagged her over and motioned for the waitress to bring another glass. Before long, the three young women had polished off the bottle and talked about ordering another. None were heavy drinkers, but the shared camaraderie had them feeling festive, and they even talked about getting up and singing a song together.

But Valentina declined more wine.

"Thanks," she said, "but no. I've got to go to Prescott in the morning and pick up Thai-ler's station wagon — they found it abandoned in the Walmart parking lot."

Alina and Malaya stared at her.

"Abandoned?" asked Malaya.

Valentina nodded. "It's been there a few days. The Prescott office talked to the Walmart employee who collected the shopping carts, and he said it had been empty morning and night — he wasn't sleeping in it as usual."

"That's a coincidence," said Alina, "we were just talking about Thai-ler and his exploration of Camilla's sinkhole. The last anyone saw Thai-ler or his vehicle was out there."

Valentina frowned. "I hate coincidences — they always point to something bad in my profession."

Malaya's face dropped. "What if he was in the sinkhole when Camelle filled it in?"

Valentina shrugged. "Well, first off, I doubt she filled it in — it was most likely her hired hand, Lars. And also, his car would still be there, not in Prescott."

"Well," added Alina, "what if someone moved it?"

Valentina shook her head. "I can't imagine Camilla doing something like that. She might not have liked those young men, but she's not devious."

The other two women stared at each other, then Alina said, "I wouldn't be so sure of that."

"I think you need to talk to her—she knows something, I'm sure of it, and I've got a bad feeling it's not good."

Valentina stared at her empty glass of wine and said, "Well, I'm off duty, and I've been drinking, so it can't be me."

Alina pushed her glass aside. "Not even unofficially? I'm no fan of Thai-ler—every day I hear more bullshit about him—but I'd hate to see Camilla get in trouble. What if she sealed him up in the sinkhole when she plugged the entrance?"

"You mean he could be trapped down there?" asked Malaya.

Valentina looked torn. Alina finally said, "Look, I'll drive us out there. It can be unofficial—but someone should find out how involved she is and ensure she didn't do something bad."

Valentina sighed. "Okay, you drive. But this is unofficial. We just ask her a few questions in a friendly visit."

Alina drove Valentina and Malaya out into the western canyons as night descended. The dragon car reflected the last red glow of the evening while on Dry Creek Road, but by the time they reached Boynton Pass and Doe Mesa, the stars had come out.

When they passed the first gate to her ranch, they noticed it was shut, and that Lars' truck was parked inside.

"I've heard that guy is a dickhead," said Alina. "Go straight to the house."

Soon, the ranch house appeared, its lower half made from cemented stone blocks, the upper portion adobe. It had a homey feel that spoke of the love the couple had shared when they built it forty years ago.

Camilla stepped onto the porch, hands on her hips, a defiant look in her eyes.

"Is Uptown Massage making house calls now?" she asked.

Alina and Malaya both blushed.

Then Camilla saw Valentina, and her eyebrows crunched together, eyes narrowing, but she held her tongue. The presence of a police officer, even one off-duty, brought on a defiant edge to her stance on the porch.

"I suppose you're here to ask me more questions about Thai-ler?" she asked Valentina.

She nodded, "I am. Do you have anything you want to tell me about him?"

Camilla perked up. "I do—he was a worthless little prick that was abusing women—that much I know."

Valentina nodded soberly. "And when was the last time you saw him?"

The old woman looked behind her at her house, then her eyes swept the yard as if seeing it for the last time. She resigned herself to her fate.

"That would be when I sealed him up in that God-forsaken hole in the ground," she spat.

The two therapists looked shocked that she admitted it out loud. Valentina shook her head. "That's cold-blooded murder," she said. "Was he conscious when you did it?"

Camilla shrugged. "Don't know—he was in too deep for me to see him. Heard him shout, though."

Valentina glanced at the other women. "He could still be alive. There's air down there, and from what I hear, they went down with proper clothing."

Suddenly, Camilla stared at Valentina and asked, "What does that mean?"

Valentina began to run towards Alina's car. "Come on, we have to see if he's still alive. If he is, you might not end up in jail."

Camilla's resolve fell away, and now she was clinging to a new hope. "Dear God," she said, "I hope we're not too late."

Chapter Ten

Water

Kita ensured her electric scooter was fully charged before driving to the western canyons. She'd got lucky with Bob and Cosmo passing by the last time and didn't want to be forced to walk back in the dark. The last traces of sunset were fading as she drove over Boynton Pass and past the Doe Mesa trailhead parking lot.

The road turned to dirt after that, rocky with a lot of dust, and she knew her scooter wouldn't do well under those conditions, so she locked it at a bike rack at the trailhead and walked from there. It was less than half a mile to Camille's ranch—and she wanted to approach it slowly and quietly anyway.

About the time she reached the ranch gate, a luminous moon was peeking over the eastern horizon. She skirted the driveway's edge, moving amongst the junipers, until she reached the sinkhole.

There was no sign of the sinkhole, only a patch of gravel where it had been. Nearby, a small John Deere mini-excavator sat parked, reflecting the moonlight.

Slowly, she scanned the area, making sure she was alone.

The night was dead, still, and silent. Not a breeze or hint of one, no crickets or cicadas, not even the occasional nightbird.

She stepped onto the gravel and walked over it, unsure what she was looking for.

When she glanced up, her heart stopped mid-beat as she saw Lars glaring at her from ten feet away.

"What the hell are you doing here!" he demanded.

Kita stared back but said nothing as she sized him up.

"Cat got your tongue?" he asked with a snarl as he pulled out his pistol and pointed it at her.

Kita raised her hands, palms visible, in a non-provoking way, and stepped slightly to the side, away from where the gun was pointed.

An owl swooped overhead, distracting Lars for a second, and Kita took that moment to step forward. She grabbed the hand that held the gun with her right hand, focusing on the thumb to break the grip. Then, as she pushed the hand away, she used her left fist to strike him in the throat.

He staggered backwards, choking and dropping the gun in the process. Kita kicked it away and took a step back.

"You little bitch!" he gasped.

As he charged forward, Kita raised the knee of her right leg, pivoted on the left foot, and delivered a fierce blow to Lars' knee, which toppled him instantly.

Before he could recover, she walked to the gun, picked it up, and tossed it into the woods.

Lars glared at her in disbelief, but as he painfully tried to stand, headlights appeared and swept across them.

Nicola, Selena and Louis had taken a while to get there. They'd picked up Louis' Buick out on Bradshaw Hill, but Boynton Pass Road turned out to be in horrible condition, and they'd been forced to use Forest Service Road 525 to retreat to Highway 89A, and then Dry Creek Road and the western canyon roads to get to Camille's ranch.

By the time they arrived, the sun had set, and a full moon had hovered over the high desert. They parked at the gate, expecting to find the spot empty, and were surprised to see Lars standing in the darkness, glaring at a young girl.

"What the hell?" exclaimed Selena.

"I'm sick of this guy," said Nicola as she hopped out and charged in his direction. "Get away from her!" she shouted, although when she got closer, she noted the girl—Kita— displayed no sign of fear.

"She attacked me!" he stammered.

Nicola looked over Kita and laughed. "Really?"

His face grew red as he realized how ridiculous that looked. "I know you," he added. "Thought I told you to fuck off."

She shook her head. "Not until I get a few answers."

Selena stepped beside her. She asked, "Where exactly was the sinkhole?"

He nodded at the area they stood in, which was distinguished only by a circle of gravel that stood out from the soft, brown soil around it. In the oncoming darkness, you could barely see the difference.

"It was right there—gone now, and I'm glad for it. No more fuckin' hippies digging it out each night."

Selena stared at it. "Did you check to see if anyone was in there when you filled it in?"

Lars suddenly looked nervous. He glanced at the house and then back at the women. He appeared to come to some inner decision and said, "I didn't fill it in."

This silenced everyone.

"That's not what we heard," said Nicola.

He shook his head. "I know. That's the story Camilla told everyone, and I backed it up—but it wasn't me. When I got here on Sunday, ready to fill it, it was as you see now."

Nicola glared at him. "Right. Then who filled it in?"

He sighed and mumbled. "I have an idea who."

The five of them stood in a circle, staring at the gravel, not speaking, until suddenly, they saw movement.

At first, it looked like a small creature was scurrying just under the surface. Then a finger appeared, and soon after, a blackened hand grasped empty air.

"What the fuck?" exclaimed Lars.

Selena rushed forward and grabbed the hand.

It desperately grasped hers, and she turned to the others.

"Oh my God!" she exclaimed. "Help me!"

Instantly, Nicola and Kita were there, digging around the hand. As they frantically tossed the gravel to the side, Lars shouted, "That's not my doing! I had nothing to do with that."

Nicola glared at him. "You knew something was up."

He guiltily looked aside, walked to his truck and returned with a shovel. Over the next few minutes, he used it, gently, to help uncover a forearm and then the entire arm.

Someone was underground, desperately trying to crawl out of the hole. Soon, a mouth appeared by the uncovered shoulder, and a voice cried out in pain and anguish, filling the night.

"I figured she filled it in," he pleaded, "but I didn't know someone was down there."

Eventually, they hauled Thai-ler to the surface. He sat there, blackened and disheveled, choking on the dirt he'd swallowed when trying to scream for help.

When Camilla's white pickup pulled up to the gate, his eyes took on a wild slant and he shouted, "That evil bitch—she did this to me!"

Camille looked as pale as a skull in the moonlight when she saw Thai-ler. She sobbed and wouldn't meet his stare. Then she leaned into Louis, buried her face in his neck, and cried.

Louis still looked disheveled, his eyes slowly scanning the scene, possibly remembering it.

Lars watched Thai-ler stand in disbelief. He said, "I can't believe you're still alive."

Thai-ler spat on the ground, his mouth still filled with dirt. Kita took her water bottle from her pack and offered it to him.

He drank it empty, then said, "I shouldn't be. All that saved me was the fact that she tossed my pack in there before filling it in, and it plugged the hole above me, about six feet down. I had some water and powerbars in it—but I've been trying to dig myself out since then."

He painfully stood and pointed a finger at her.

"I'm gonna make sure you do time for this."

Now, Valentina stepped forward. She was in civilian clothes, and Thai-ler didn't know she was a police officer, but the confidence in her voice calmed him.

"I think what's more important right now is we get you some medical help."

"How long have I been down there?" he asked, still not believing he was free.

Lars stared at the whole and said, "Three or four days—I don't know."

The women glared at him, and he added, "I moved his car—okay, I admit that—but I didn't know he was in the fuckin' hole. I figured he was off screwin' around, and it might deter him if his vehicle disappeared for a while. I knew they would find it at Walmart."

Thai-ler was coming around. He glared at Camille. "I don't need a hospital—I want to go to the station right now and press charges."

Malaya suddenly stood before him and said, "Me too! I want to file a report."

He froze as he stared at her, suddenly recognizing her and remembering their last encounter.

Selena stood by her side and said, "I also want to file a report."

Now Thai-ler looked uncertain. He didn't recognize Selena, but he could see the anger contained within her petite frame.

Valentina said, "Why don't we all cool down. Let's get you some medical attention first, and tomorrow I will get an officer to talk to you. Can you live with that?"

He stared at Malaya and Selena, and then slowly nodded.

Valentina paused. "You shouldn't bring him to the Cottonwood hospital unless you want a report filed."

Louis perked up. "I know a guy," and dialed Dr. Jason.

Valentina nodded. "Okay, we will pick this up tomorrow."

Courthouse Butte

THURSDAY

Epilogue

Wood

*L*ouis was dancing with Cosmo only a few days after he'd spent a night on Cockscomb. He no longer seemed wobbly, and holding the baby seemed to calm him. Still, they gripped each other tightly, entwined like two dragons, as if they were both afraid Louis might drop the infant.

Bob smiled at the scene, glad they still managed to move to the music. Bob had been dancing since the sixties, and he always enjoyed watching Louis' erratic dance. He didn't have a lot of rhythm, but he certainly seemed to enjoy it.

The weekly ecstatic dance at the Sun & Moon Studio was one of Louis' favorite events. He'd begun dancing there six months before, surprised to find he liked dancing after avoiding it most of his life. When he woke that morning, he had stumbled to it like it was any other day, his night in the wilderness forgotten.

Bob and his daughter, Trina, were on either side of him and the baby, swaying to a slow, melodic track with a tinge of the Middle East to the music. The DJ, Amelia, was originally from Australia and blessed dancers with her melodic visions once a month, having done so for nearly twenty years.

Veronica and Selena took up the middle of the dance floor, moving in tandem to their own beat. At one point, they circled Louis and Cosmo and extended their hands as if absorbing some baby magic. Over by the wall, Frankie danced by herself, her vibrant pink hair flashing as she moved. The room had about thirty people in it, all of them dancing, all of them sharing a moment.

While he danced, Louis thought about the last few days and how, despite the craziness, everything had returned to normal. Kita was back in class, suffering her way through another day of middle school. Alina was working at Uptown Massage, but she had texted her plans to attend a drum circle that night. And Nicola had headed back to Mesa with the sunrise, claiming she'd had "enough of us Sedona people" for a while.

Eventually, Louis stepped outside to catch his breath. He nodded at Malaya on his way out. She was working the door, collecting money or checking off those who had prepaid.

She said, "Hey, Thai-ler is out there—he tried to sneak in, but I called him out. Said he didn't have any money, so I didn't let him in—nobody wants him in here, anyway."

Louis glanced across the parking lot and saw him. He looked like death warmed over and not fit for dancing.

"What the hell is he doing here, anyway?" he asked.

Malaya shrugged. "I guess this is where Officer Valentina arranged to meet him."

Louis sat on the bench outside and watched the young man fidget uncomfortably in the shadow of the building, about thirty feet away. The dance was winding down, nearing the point that the music would end, and everyone would gather in a circle and share their impressions of the event.

A few people avoided that part of the ceremony and snuck out. The first was Selena, who sat next to Louis and gave him a warm smile. The next was Frankie, who winked at him as she walked past.

Frankie had finally finished renovating a school bus and was about to embark on a cross-country drive. It had a small wood stove, a bathtub in the back and all her other dreams incorporated into the vehicle. Her two dogs waited there now, one with its head poked out the window.

Selena asked casually, "So, Louis, any plans tonight?"

He shrugged, "Not really. Might just stay home and read."

She shook her head. "Ha. I don't believe that for a minute."

He raised his hands defensively. "Why not?"

She gave him a knowing look. "Because the moon will be full tonight and I know how you are with full moons."

"Oh yeah, the Beaver Moon," he grinned, then fibbed. "I'd forgotten about it. Are you afraid I'm gonna run off to Cockscomb again?"

She nodded. "A little."

"And what are you doing?" he asked.

She smiled. "I'd like to go to the drum circle at Yavapai Vista, unless you want me to check in on you."

"You know," began Louis, "Alina said she's going to that as well — maybe I'll go there."

Selena looked relieved. "Good, I will see you there. It's the last of four supermoons this year, and I didn't want to miss it."

She stood and hugged him. "I've got to run, I'm only on my lunch break from the Dragon's Den. I'll see you at Yavapai Vista!"

As she walked away, a police car driven by Officer Valentina pulled up.

Thai-ler left the shadowed safety of the wall and walked over. He looked down at the car and asked, "Where's my station wagon? I thought you were going to bring it to me."

Valentina shook her head. "Nope, but I'll bring you to it."

He shook his head, "Then I have to drive all the way back here — that's a bit inconvenient."

The officer shook her head. "You won't be coming back to Sedona. You're finished here."

Thai-ler puffed up his chest. "After how I was handled, I expected better treatment—maybe even some compensation."

She stared at him for a beat, watching.

Finally, she said, "This morning, I arrived at the station to find that a half-dozen other women had filed complaints about you. You're lucky I'm letting you leave town at all."

He looked shocked. "I haven't done anything! This is a witch hunt. You know it, or you wouldn't let me go."

Valentina smiled at him, but there was nothing kind in her smile. "Oh, I'm not through with you at all. I'm planning on watching you for a while, and I'll be in touch with the authorities wherever you go—one complaint filed by any woman you are connected to, and I'll be coming for you."

Thai-ler stood there, not sure what to do.

The dance ended, and everyone filed outside, but then stood there staring at Thai-ler poised before the cruiser. Suddenly, all the happy smiles faded as the group stared down the young man. They'd all heard about his treatment of the women in town by then, and nobody was sympathetic.

Bob stood there with Cosmo, who again pointed west, as if saying it was time for him to go.

Someone shouted, "Adios, Thigh-ler," but nobody laughed.

Then Frankie pulled up in her bus to wave goodbye to everyone. She lived out of town and hadn't heard any of the gossip concerning Thai-ler.

He looked her over, then leaned down to Officer Valentina and said, "What if I find my own ride?"

She shrugged, "Do whatever you want."

Frankie had two doors to the vehicle, but she kept the old one used to pick up kids for school because she could control it from the driver's seat.

She slid the door open.

"Goodbye, my lovelies," she said to everyone. "I'm off to Prescott to get a part, then who knows where—maybe I'll see you in the fall."

Thai-ler put on his best smile and tried to look charming.

"Hey, I've got to get to Prescott," he said. "Mind if I catch a lift?"

Frankie was a good judge of character. She looked him up and down, then grabbed a lever and, before slamming the door shut, said coldly, "Fuck no!"

Everyone cheered her on as she sped away.

Sedona Dragons

110

Sedona Places Mentioned in this Book

Amitabha Stupa and Peace Park (The Stupa)

Sedona Hot Yoga

The Chocola Tree Organic Oasis Restaurant

Berry Divine

Uptown Massage

The Barbara Antonson Memorial Park (The Pavilion)

Hiro's Sushi & Japanese Kitchen

The Dragon's Den

Tortas del Fuego

Vino di Sedona - *Thursday night open mike*

Sun Moon Studio - *Sunday Ecstatic Dance*

Yavapai Vista - *Full Moon & Tuesday Ecstatic Dances*

Author's Note

Last year, after a significant life change, I decided to lean into what made me uncomfortable. I reformed my diet and exercise habits. I also began dancing—first ecstatic, then Latin—and then public speaking. I wasn't ready to date, so instead, I went on non-romantic dates about once a week. This was such a breath of fresh air, just going out with someone because I was genuinely interested in them—not with a physical or relationship goal at the end. I went out with people from 30 to 70, and truly enjoyed their company and the time we spent together. This allowed me to meet all sorts of women, and in Sedona, many of them were facilitators of some kind. By coincidence—or not—many were also dragons. In the end, like many other writers, it all worked its way into a story.

Acknowledgments

As this is my eleventh novel, I've got some good systems in place and some pretty cool locations to call my office. I wrote the first half of this novella in Rome, in a cheap hotel called the *Marco Polo*, just a block from Termini Station. The second half I wrote in Australia, while staying with my good friends, Steve and Sally Douglas. Drew Holman helped by creating another great cover for me.

Special thanks to: Alyssa Portrey, Martika DeMayo, Dr. Jason Wesley, Jenn Richards of Hot Yoga, Malaya Ellsmore, Ryan Morton of the Dragon's Den, and John & Mason Bradshaw.

Gratitude to Masafumi "Cham" Hasegawa, of Hiro's Sushi, for fielding my countless questions about dragons whenever I ate there. Thank you, Rick Koehler, of the Sedona Karate studio, for your help in choreographing the fight between Kita and Lars. Thanks to Bob Brill for his eagle eyes and edits on early drafts, and also to Claire Obermarck for her help with some of this when it was just a tale or an unwritten story.

A special thanks to those who helped me dance and get out of my head--I would still be a mess without your help. Thank you: Veronica Marconi, Sabrina Malinalli, Tikisha Nelson, Gabriel BE, Mary Dancer, Amalia Camateros, Gwen Payne, Austin Crawford, Teany Hidalgo, and so many more.

Robert Louis DeMayo and Roman.

Biography

Robert Louis DeMayo is a native of Hollis, N.H., but lived in many corners of the planet before settling in the Southwest. He took up writing at age twenty when he left his job as a biomedical engineer to explore the world. In the last decade before the internet, he visited nearly 100 countries, crossing many overland.

His extensive journaling during these travels — and many more after — inspired four of his novels and far-reaching work for the travel section of *The Telegraph*, out of Nashua, NH, as well as the *Hollis Times*. He is a long-time member of The Explorers Club and Chair of its Southwest Chapter.

His undying hunger for exploration led to a job marketing for Eos Study Tours, a company that served as a travel office for six non-profit organizations and offered dives to the *Titanic* and the *Bismarck*, Antarctic voyages, African safaris and archaeological tours throughout the world.

For several years after that, Robert worked as a tour guide in Alaska and the Yukon during the summers and as a jeep guide in Arizona during the winter. He was made general manager of the Jeep tour company, but eventually left the guiding world to write full-time.

DeMayo is the author of **ten** novels: *The Making of Theodore Roosevelt*, a fictionalized account of Roosevelt´s first acquaintance with wilderness living; *The Light Behind Blue Circles*, a mystery thriller set in Africa; *The Wayward Traveler*, a semi-autobiographical story following a young traveler on his adventures abroad; *The Legend of Everett Ruess*, a fictionalized account of the life and times of the young solo traveler of the American West; *The Road to Sedona*, the story of a young family that heads up to Alaska to find work in the wake of 9/11; *The Sirens of Oak Creek*, a historical mystery of Oak Creek Canyon, Arizona spanning twelve centuries.

Plus *Pithecophilia*, a collection of stories of ape encounters, and *The King of the Coral Sea*, a historical fiction account of Michael Fomenko's great sea journey.

In November 2024, he published *American Literary Nomads*, called "a modern version of Steinbeck's *Travels with Charlie*." Most recently, he published *Aroostook Dreams*, a historical mystery set in northern Maine. Collectively, his books have won a dozen national awards.

He currently resides in Sedona, AZ, and spends his time with his three daughters, Tavish Lee, Saydrin Scout, and Martika Louise.

Books by Robert Louis DeMayo

Nonfiction Travelogue

The Wayward Traveler
(978-0983345398)

The Road to Sedona
(978-0991118359)

Pithecophilia
(978-0998439181)

American Literary Nomads
(979-8989343003)

Historical Fiction

The Making of Theodore Roosevelt
(978-0983345312)

The Legend of Everett Ruess
(978-099118311)

The King of the Coral Sea
(978-0998439198)

Historical Mysteries

The Light Behind Blue Circles
(978-0983345350)

The Sirens of Oak Creek
(978-0998439136)

Aroostook Dreams
(979-8989343010)

Sedona Dragons
(979-8991819770)

Poetry & Prose

Random Thoughts from the Road
(978-0983345343)

The Sirens of Oak Creek

Historical Mystery
Wayward Publishing
Available in print & eBook

*"This was a great story! I want to read the entire thing over
again to catch details I may have missed in rushing to learn "what
happens next?!" The lure of the cave is irresistible to the men who
seek out its power, and generations of women guarding it through
time are powerless to save the men from its secrets. Wave after wave,
time circles back, lessons are learned and forgotten, but cultures are
linked by shared geography in an a remote, ageless canyon. It was
fun to experience it through each
set of fresh eyes and ears."*

Lynn Perry

Also by *Robert Louis DeMayo*

THE SIRENS OF OAK CREEK

A hidden, sacred canyon. Eight women. Twelve centuries. And a mystical song that connects it all.

Deep in the wilderness lies a hidden canyon, one that calls out to travelers with its haunting siren song. Sacred wisdom, terrible secrets, and a veil of mystery shroud it - but the power of nature cannot be ignored.

Seen through the eyes of eight women across time, Sedona's Oak Creek Canyon calls through the ages, echoing across twelve centuries to capture the minds of visitors from ancient hunter-gatherers to Spanish conquistadors to modern-day seekers of truth.

Though these women bear witness to nature's magic, their sacred guardianship is matched only by the ill-fated curiosity of the men who seek to unravel the canyon's secrets. As time crashes on, one wave after another, cultures are linked, and stories remain unbroken as this lost, ageless canyon brings myths to life and fuels the folklore of generations.

From award-winning, best-selling author Robert Louis DeMayo, *The Sirens of Oak Creek* is a gripping novel that artfully intertwines local myth with historical fact, carrying timeless themes that reflect the power of nature, magic, and immaterial realms.

Please enjoy this short excerpt from *The Sirens of Oak Creek*

Random Chapter

800 A.D.
(October)

I was up before dawn the morning the strangers arrived —
everyone was up! These would be the first visitors from the
southern people we'd had in many years.

My mother was very busy, and I quickly hurried out of her
way. She barely acknowledged my departure because she knew
I'd be with everyone else, crowded along the creek where the
southern trail passed, hoping to get a glimpse of the visitors
when they arrived. They called themselves the People of the
Corn, although, in later days, they were known as the Mayans.

On my way through our courtyard, where some of our best
fabrics were now on display, I overheard some gossip about
problems the last time the People of the Corn had visited. None
of it interested me until I heard them mention a bear attack, and
my blood froze.

I was terrified of bears.

I rushed along, checking every dark shadow on the descent
down to the creek. In the verdant coolness along the water's
edge, I finally shook off the image.

Long before most of the villagers arrived, I climbed an old
sycamore whose thick pale limbs stretched over the path along
the creek.

And then I waited with the birds.

Above me, a black and white flicker pecked his way into a
dead branch, looking for insects. And below, a quail called out
mournfully, alarmed when other spectators arrived, settling too
close to its nest.

As the first golden rays of the sun crested the rim of our
valley, the strangers appeared in the distance along the

riverbank. They came from the west with the rising sun lighting their faces.

I counted eight in the group: five men who seemed to act as guards and porters, two female retainers, and a high-ranking woman. Two of the men led the way. Wearing mantles decorated with bones and exotic feathers, they hefted their shields high but smiled as they marched, making it known that they came as friends.

The men were covered with tattoos and piercings, and their dress was so outlandish—so otherworldly—that for a few brief moments, all I could do was peer through the green foliage and gawk.

Behind the two in the front walked a mountain of a man with bulging muscles, a stout spear, and a severe and untrusting stare. He wore a spotted pelt over his shoulders, and later the men—having never seen a jaguar—argued about what kind of animal it came from.

Even the porters, who wore only loincloths, had strange piercings and sported ornaments made from jade or obsidian.

When they passed underneath me, I saw the important, white-haired woman whose stately gait and regal expression seemed to underscore her importance.

Vibrant quetzal feathers bounced in tight circles over her head, seemingly floating above her. Beautiful blue flowers decorated her dress. Her entire appearance took my breath away.

I was always around the women, and in our tribe, they took great pride in the fashioning of textiles. They made beautiful cloth, and our designs were sought after; but the craftsmanship and colors of *her* clothing were so exotic, so brilliant, they seemed to be plucked from a dream.

There flashed at me reds and blues and greens that were so vivid I had never seen them captured in cloth or on pottery before. It was like a cardinal had given up its secret and handed over its red color, or maybe it was the blue from the belly of an insect, or all the colors of the sunset. They were all there, and in

126

the quick glimpse I got from the tree, I felt all the colors I'd known up to that point slowly fading.

They dulled even the reds in Itzel's feathers — back when he had feathers.

The woman seemed to have to balance her head ornaments carefully but still somehow managed to glimpse me above her.

Ever-so-slightly, she tilted her head up and winked at me.

I almost fell out of the tree, and she seemed to suppress a smile.

Sedona Dragons

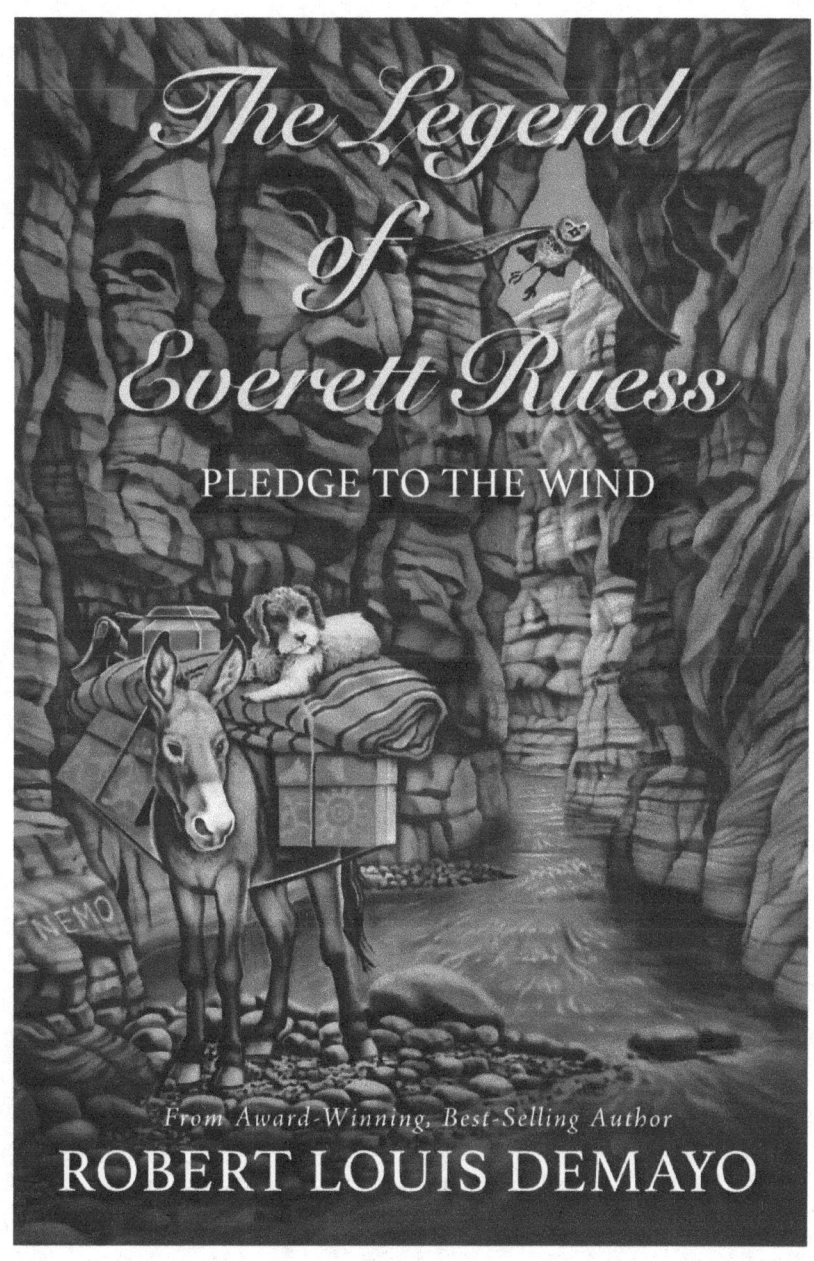

Everett Ruess, Curly and a burrow named Chocolatero.
(Drawing by Tom Fish)

Also by **Robert Louis DeMayo**

THE LEGEND OF EVERETT RUESS

In this compelling narrative, DeMayo has taken journal excerpts, poems, and letters Everett sent to family and friends in the early thirties and turned them into historical fiction. Through this recreation of Everett's travels, we are given rare glimpses of the young artist as he traveled the southwest—much of which was still an unexplored wilderness back then.

Everett traveled alone, accompanied only by a dog named Curly, but he often stayed with Navajo or Hopi. Using only burros or horses, Everett explored much of Utah and Arizona, covering about twenty miles a day. He crossed the Grand Canyon regularly. The Navajo and Hopi who came across him, miles from any road, thought he was a mystic and called him Picture Man. They allowed him to witness— and participate in—ceremonies that today are mostly off-limits to non-Indians.

Upon reading it, Brian Ruess wrote, "In this work of fiction ... I saw Everett for the first time, as he might actually have been."

Historical Fiction.
Wayward Publishing.
Available in print, eBook
& audiobook.

"This novel affirms the saying that 'all who wander are not lost.' The portrayal of Everett Ruess gives us a beautiful, poetic adventure. We sense his desire to be at one with nature and how this becomes his true spiritual home – and perhaps his ultimate resting place. It is a gripping tale that any traveler or explorer will relate to and enjoy."

Sally Douglas

The Narrows, Zion National Park

Please enjoy this short excerpt from *The Legend of Everett Ruess*:

Random Chapter

The Hole-in-the-Rock Trail, Utah
(October 1934)

*E*verett led Cockleburs and Chocolatero over a rocky mesa of sage and snakeweed. They were on an open plain cut by deep ravines, following the Hole-in-the-Wall Trail as it ran south by southeast out of Escalante.

A cold breeze greeted him, and he had his head down.

The Mormon trailblazers who had created this trail had eventually stopped at the town of Bluff, one hundred and eighty miles from Escalante. Everett's destination as he entered this remote wilderness was the Colorado River, about sixty miles away. To his right lay the Kaiparowits Plateau, whose steep canyons drained into the Escalante, and directly south was Glen Canyon.

Late in the afternoon he came upon a gentle stream that flowed by the base of a sandstone cliff, and he prepared camp. "This place looks like it was made for us," he told the burros as he unloaded the saddle and kyacks.

Above them, a towering wall of rock lit up orange and yellow in the afternoon sun. Tall pines grew by the stream and sprouted on the cliff face wherever a small shelf had collected soil. Far up on the top of the wall, he could see stunted, twisted pines that were now highlighted in gold as the sun set.

He made a small fire, boiled water for rice, and tethered the burros with enough lead to move but not get into trouble. He hadn't seen another human since setting foot on the trail, only squirrels, lizards and birds, and he relaxed by the fire, enjoying his solitude.

Later, the fire had died down to glowing embers, and he decided to write in his journal. He sat with it on his lap, watching the night, listening to it breathe around him.

He was about to jot down an entry when he heard Navajo chanting.

It was far off, barely discernible over the chirping of the crickets that lived along the stream. He thought of the young Navajos he had encountered a few nights before.

He leaned forward, opening his ears more. Cockleburs shifted by his side, and he shushed him.

Then it came again. There was only one singer. The song seemed muffled, and he couldn't make it out, but the hair on the back of his neck stood up. He felt sure it was one used against witches...

Snoopy Rock